THE ROOK

[this novel is dedicated to a great many people,
but most notably, Jay, Alexus, and my family]

CHAPTER ONE

Because There's **Beauty** In The **Breakdown**

It all started with the rook.

"Excuse me," he interrupted uncertainly, adjusting his glasses with a nervous smile, "Don't you mean it started with the *shipwreck*?"

"No, it started with the rook, it all started with the rook! Nothing was wrong before the rook everything was normal dark but normal but the rook made things wrong and he—"

"Calm down! Please." The psychologist adjusted his glasses again, using the movement to try to surreptitiously wipe sweat from his brow. This patient was new, and he was nervous because of it. His tension wasn't missed, however. He felt the glare. "I believe you. Did the rook come before or after the shipwreck?"

"...After."

"Tell me about the shipwreck first, then, if you'd please. You can tell me about the rook when you get to... him."

"Okay. It started with the rook, but before that, the ship went down. I don't know why it did..." The patient messed with a silver charm bracelet, twirling it around a thin wrist. The psychologist wrote the observation down on his clipboard. "My parents were on the ship. Mom had gotten a lifejacket for herself and for me. I think dad had one, too, but he lost his—maybe he gave it away—he'd do that—"

"Take a deep breath, and then continue."

The order was followed. "Dad was telling us to get to the lifeboats. He was going back, but... I don't know why. I don't know why any of that had to happen. Why *did* it have to happen?! We had just wanted to go on a vacation, and instead—"

Michael Sante was lifted bodily and held out over the edge

of the boat. He stared down in terror at the water so far below. The boat lurched and he nearly fell out, but the man helping them into the lifeboat caught him. Heart pounding, he turned back fearfully to where his mother was helping a little girl over the edge.

"Mom."

One word. One simple word, pathetically called, and that was all the beckoning she needed. Little girl nestled safely into the boat, his mother climbed carefully over the railing and stepped over towards their rescue. Michael leaned against her, taking comfort in her presence beside him. The boat behind them lurched again, this time accompanied by a horrible scraping sound. The flames that had been creeping stealthily along before were now rushing to find more fuel. People started screaming—as if they weren't before.

The world suddenly got a lot quieter as hands firmly covered his ears. Michael looked up, but his head was turned and buried in his mother's shoulder instead.

"Where's dad?" he asked, voice muffled by her shirt.

She took her hands off his ears and instead concentrated on smoothing back his blonde hair from his forehead. "He'll be coming. He just had to make sure your uncle and aunt were okay."

The lifeboat hit the water and they started to row away from the sinking ship. Another explosion came, however, and upset the little vessel. Michael's mother was tipped overboard, inadvertently tugging her son along with her. A couple others were in the water as well, splashing and spluttering. The water wasn't terribly cold, but it was still hard to breathe in the lifejacket and the sudden shock of it.

Michael turned around, seeing their lifeboat on fire. "Come on, Michael, this way, there's an island just over there—!" He turned again to where his mother was pointing. The island just over there was far away. Very far away. Just a speck, really, on the horizon. But with the ship on fire and the lifeboat on fire and people screaming and chaos and everything going wrong, so very wrong, he had to swim—

"Please calm down," he insisted, almost begged. The patient took a deep breath and tried to stop the hands connected to the jingling, silver charm bracelet from shaking. It wasn't the other way around; it was the hands that were connected to the bracelet, not the bracelet connected to the hands. The wrist existed to support the hands to continue twirling the bracelet. The psychologist cleared his throat (and his mind), glanced down at the clipboard, and tried again to detach himself from the patient. He said softly, "Why don't we talk about something else right now? You can tell me about the shipwreck later. Tell me about your vacation up until that point."

"It was... fun. We took a flight to Florida, and that's where the ship left from. It was really warm and I spent a lot of time on the deck. I hadn't ever been on a ship before." The words seemed forced, contrived, mechanical. The patient was still calming down, though, so the psychologist tried not to dwell on that. "...I had met them on the ship. Tuesday and Mr. Silvermin. I had stood on the railing next to Tuesday when we first left, and we sat at the same table as Mr. Silvermin to eat dinner that night."

"Tell me about them." The psychologist hoped the relief didn't show in his voice to get to a less upsetting topic.

"Mr. Silvermin was always polite. He and my dad talked about business during dinner. He seemed very responsible. Respectable. He tried to take care of us, too, on the island."

"Tried to?"

"…" The silence was suddenly too thick and too heavy. The psychologist sighed, adjusted his glasses, and scribbled something out on his clipboard. Dark eyes watched him.

"Anything else about him?"

"He had reddish-brown hair and a mustache—"

"About his personality, not his looks. I have seen a photograph of Mr. Silvermin and know what he looks like." He smiled, trying to reassure his patient. Not that anything could do that, oh no, not after everything that happened. Still, it was worth a shot. You had to go through the motions, even if the motions wouldn't help.

"He's very smart and tries very hard to do the right thing," came the perfectly toneless reply. The psychologist frowned.

"I know what you mean by that, but…"

"I… I don't know what to say about him. I'm sorry that I don't. I never really interacted much with him, never got to know him very well. I know he's a businessman, he has a bit of an accent, and he feels responsible for what happened. That's all."

"Do you think he's responsible for what happened?"

The air in the room got impossibly heavier. The psychologist stood his ground on this one; he had to find out something other than a story for this session. He had to try to fix the damage that had been done, and the first step to that was having the patient admit to certain feelings.

Finally, the answer came in a very small, very meek, "No."

"Why not?"

"He didn't do anything wrong!"

The psychologist wrote that down. Peeking over the edge of his clipboard, he tried to figure out how to approach the situation once more. "…Tell me about Tuesday now."

"She… I don't know about her."

"You have to know *something* about her."

"I don't."

"Come now, you don't have any opinion whatsoever?"

"I… I don't know what to say about her! She's—she's just so—she's the one who suggested it in the first place!" The shouted words hung in the room as if there'd been an echo. The psychologist didn't have to write that down; he would never forget those words or the accompanying expression for as long as he lived.

For the first time, he tried to think of this not as another case, but as the tragedy it really was.

"…Do you not like Tuesday?"

"…She was nice to me. I liked her."

"That was past tense. Was it meant to be?"

"I… like her. She was kind and told me stories. We would lie on the sand together and she would tell me fairytales and stuff. She tried to tell me the story of *Hamlet* once, but it didn't come out very well."

"So… you liked these stories?"

"Yes. I did."

"But you still hold bitter feelings?"

"I… A bit… But… She suggested it, so it was her fault, wasn't it? It was all her fault?" The question ended in a high voice, the patient staring up at the psychologist with eyes that begged for an excuse, any excuse. Any excuse in the world to assuage the guilt and create an answer that could be taken as the gospel truth.

So the psychologist did the only thing he could in that situation without making things irreparably worse. "I thought you said it was all the rook's fault," he replied mildly.

His patient's face fell. It was not the proper answer, not that had been looked for at any rate, but it was the only one that would ever be received from a decent human being.

"...Tell me, how many of you made it to that island?"

"There were four of us. Mr. Silvermin, Tuesday, myself, and my dad."

The psychologist's head snapped up in surprise. He hadn't heard that part before. "Your father? Then... What happened to your father?"

The dull, forced responses were back. "He swam out to save someone who was drowning. He didn't come back."

"Dad, don't, don't do it! Come back!" Michael pulled on his father's arm insistently, rapidly nearing tears.

"For God's sake, man, I'll do it!" Silvermin protested, walking with them both down to the edge of the beach.

"Don't worry about me." He was already kicking off his shoes and taking off his jacket. He turned and smiled at Michael reassuringly, ruffling his hair. "You know I'm a good swimmer, don't you? I'll be back in just a minute!"

Michael finally started crying, letting go in favor of wiping the tears away. His father strode away, Silvermin following and hissing things under his breath. Just off the shore, the splashing could be heard getting weaker, the shouting coming in intermittent periods.

"Look! She's drowning! I'll be *right back*!" Michael's father finally snapped at Silvermin. The red-haired man looked slightly taken aback and did nothing further to try to dissuade him from swimming back out into the ocean. Michael ran towards his father, but he was already wading out into the sea. Silvermin held out an arm and caught the boy, dragging him back so he wouldn't pursue him.

"Don't worry, your father will be right back," he said quietly, watching.

"Dad, come back!"

He didn't.

"...He was a brave man. He died trying to save another's life," the psychologist said quietly.

He expected anger, or bitterness, or perhaps even tears. All he got was, "He didn't have to go."

"Would you have let the woman drown?"

"...No. Mr. Silvermin would have gone, though! Why couldn't he have let *him* go—?!"

"I can't pretend to know what happened, or his motives, or his thoughts at the time. I'm sorry. I'm sure he would have loved nothing more than to return to you, but he had to go out and try to save the woman."

"...He was hoping it was mom," the patient said listlessly, staring down at the silver charm bracelet.

"Then can you really blame him?"

"He left me! He left me for a chance—"

"A chance to bring your family back together. Wouldn't that have been worth it?" He received no reply, but it wasn't as if he had been expecting one. He jotted down a few more notes on the situation on his clipboard, and then looked back up at the patient sitting across from him. "...Tell me how the island went *before* you met the rook."

"I-I-I—"

"Shh, shh, it's okay."

"He-He—"

"It's okay, it's okay," she murmured, brushing back his hair like his mother had.

It was nearing sundown, and no one else had shown up on the island. His father hadn't come back, and the woman he'd been trying to save hadn't appeared, either. It was just the three of them on the island, alone.

Michael was being rocked as he cried. The brown-haired girl was doing it, trying to act motherly. He needed it, but it didn't mean he liked it. Only his mother should be doing this— but if she were, then he wouldn't be in the situation in the first place...

"Wh-Why did this happen," he whispered, voice hoarse.

"I don't know," she replied softly, rubbing his shoulders. "It's terrible though, isn't it?"

"Yeah."

"You know, let's just go to sleep. It's getting dark, and maybe they'll show up in the morning," she continued in that same quiet, soothing voice.

"I-I know th-they won't!" he wailed. With that, Michael started crying again, started sobbing, unable to stop himself. He had never cried so much in his life before. Then again, his life just hours before seemed so foreign to him now. He had been *happy* then.

"You don't know that, shh. Some people really do show up the next morning. Haven't you ever seen *Titanic*? Look at how long they were out there for."

Standing a little ways away, the businessman cleared his throat. "Bad example," he remarked. She gave him a look, but soon turned her attention back to Michael.

"Let's just go to sleep now, since we have nothing else to do. Things will be better in the morning. ...Would you like a story?" She smoothed back his hair again, smiling. The silver charm bracelet on her wrist sparkled in the fading light. Michael nodded miserably, sniffling. "Well, let's see. Once upon a time, there was this dog and a cat. They always, *always* fought…"

Michael wasn't sure at what point he fell asleep, but he never did find out what happened to the dog and the cat. He didn't dream or wake up at all during the night, so the next time he opened his eyes, all he knew was that it was bright out, he was stiff, he was hungry, and he had a headache.

He sat up and propped himself up with an elbow, rubbing his eyes with his free hand. He felt horrible. Unfortunately, he soon remembered why. He sat fully up and started taking deep breaths to try to stop himself from crying. Things would look better in the morning, right? And maybe his parents had shown up in the night!

Michael clambered to his feet, and, after stretching, started to investigate the beach. There was no one in sight, which was saying something, because he could see a *lot*. The beach spread out on his right and left almost endlessly, and the sea lay in front of him, equally vast. Behind him, however, was the forest.

He started walking towards it, looking for other footprints, but found none. Instead, he found green. There were grasses, ferns, bizarre plants and trees all around. Having lived in Colorado for all of his life, Michael was definitely unprepared for a tropical habitat.

"…if we just climb it—"

"And how do you propose doing that easily?"

Michael turned when he heard voices. They were immediately recognizable as Tuesday and Silvermin, however, dashing any hope he had of seeing his parents again. Just the thought of that brought stinging tears back to his eyes. Wiping them away with his wrist, he clambered through the undergrowth in the direction of the voices. Not too far away, the girl and man were standing under a large palm tree, staring up at it.

Tuesday was the first to notice him, breaking out into a

wide smile when she did. "Look! We found coconuts."

"We just need to get the blasted things down, now..." Silvermin added, mostly to himself.

Michael looked around. A lot of the trees looked like the one in front of them, but now that he was *really* looking, it seemed as that not all of them had coconuts. "...Why can't we just climb the tree?" he asked, sniffing back the last vestiges of his tears.

Tuesday's smile dimmed a couple watts. "Well, there are no branches to climb with, for one. And the bark is really rough and scratchy, so whoever climbs it would probably cut themselves pretty badly."

"I've climbed trees before," Michael said as he stepped closer to the tree. "I'm good at it."

"Have you ever climbed a palm tree before?" Silvermin asked, nodding at the tree. "They're a different sort of animal."

"Tree," he corrected, patting the trunk. It *was* pretty rough, but he didn't think it was too bad. Not that much worse than regular tree bark, anyway. "I could climb this—"

"If you fall, or cut yourself, or hurt yourself, we can't just go to the hospital," Tuesday cut in nervously, shifting her weight to her other leg. "That's what we're worried about. Even a little cut or scrape could get infected, and then that would be bad."

"We'll be able to get to a hospital later, though. When we get rescued." Michael hadn't really thought about them being shipwrecked before, or stranded on an apparently deserted island, but it was true. All they could do was wait for someone to come, pick them up, and take them back home. So that meant that they were on their own until then... "Do we have gloves or something? If we cover my hands, then I won't get scraped."

Tuesday and Silvermin looked at each other. "I don't have any gloves," she said as the man shook his head.

"I have my jacket, and that would protect your arms, though. The sleeves should be long enough to cover your hands…" He took off his jacket and held it out for Michael. True to his word, it dwarfed the boy. The sleeves easily covered his hands—and then some. "See? Ingenuity at its finest."

Michael smiled, the first time in quite awhile. He jumped when Silvermin picked him up. "Wha—?"

"It may only be a couple feet, but it's a boost nonetheless," he replied briskly, setting him on his shoulders with a grunt. "See if that doesn't help you."

"An-And don't worry, we'll catch you if you fall!" Tuesday added, circling the trunk anxiously.

After the problem of the rough trunk was solved, however—even if Michael could do nothing but worry about his hands and if he were to get hurt and get infected—getting to the top was easy. He had to hug the tree with one arm while he pried the coconuts off, which was a little difficult at first, but he soon got the hang of it. A couple of the coconuts nearly hit the pair below, too, but even that was easily taken care of as they watched from afar.

"I'm coming back down!" he called. He had gotten all but the two toughest ones off the tree and figured that that would be enough for some food. At least for a little while. He didn't know how long they were going to be on the island, but surely, it wouldn't be that long. He wasn't sure about eating nothing but coconuts for any amount of time.

"Wait! Can you see if you can get a couple of the leaves off as well?" Silvermin shouted back up. He earned two confused looks in response. "Palm leaves can be used for a lot of things. Beds, for starters, and green leaves tend to smoke when burned. We'll need to start a signal fire at some point today."

It only took a few moments of wrestling with the leaves,

however, for Michael to discover that it would be too hard to get them off the tree. "I can't! They're too tough!"

"It's fine! We'll just find ones already on the ground!" Tuesday chirped, beckoning him back down.

After managing to find some bananas as well, the trio settled down on the beach to eat and discuss. Or rather, Silvermin discussed, Tuesday tried to offer some help, and Michael listened. They decided that food and water had to be a priority. They had enough food for the rest of the day, but they only had what liquid was inside the coconuts and seawater for water. (Actually, only the coconut water. Michael had suggested drinking the seawater and was immediately and rather harshly shot down by both of the others. Apparently it was bad to drink.)

Among the three of them, they had very little. The clothes on their backs, Silvermin had an old Swiss army knife that was a little dull and hadn't been used properly in years, Tuesday had pockets full of gum, candy wrappers, and a cell phone ruined by the seawater, and the lifejackets Michael and Tuesday had been wearing was all that they possessed. Everything else was in the ocean.

"...Buck up! Everything will be alright. We'll start a fire, make a bit of a shelter, shall we? And before you know it, rescue will be coming and picking us up and we'll be back to civilization before we know it!" Silvermin exclaimed, clasping his hands together. Tuesday and Michael continued eating their bananas, cheerless and mute. "Alright then... You two stay here, and, er, start building a pit or something along those lines for a fire. I will go see if I can't find anything else a little further inland. Stay here on the beach, alright?"

"Okay, Mr. Silvermin," Tuesday replied quietly, glancing back at the trees behind her.

The man traipsed off. Michael watched him go. Tuesday

was more focused on her silver charm bracelet. She twisted it a couple times on her wrist, then sighed, setting her hands on her feet as she drew her knees up to her chest.

Michael turned so that he could look at the sparkling water. "...Do people show up on the second day?" he asked after too long of a silence. She looked up at him.

It took her too long to create the necessary reassuring smile for the situation. "Sure, of course they do," she said. Michael knew better, though; she had told him the truth before she'd even opened her mouth. He blinked a couple times to make sure the tears wouldn't come again, took another bite of his banana, and continued looking out at the water.

His parents weren't coming back.

CHAPTER TWO

You Can Fool Yourself, **I Promise It Will Help**

Michael stared into the fire, somewhat mesmerized by the dancing flames. Tuesday had already told him several times not to do that, but he honestly couldn't help it. If he stared at the fire, he didn't have to think. Instead, he could simply stare and let his mind shut off for a little bit.

Too much had happened in such a short time. It was all beginning to come home for the boy, too. He was just now realizing, truly *realizing*, that his parents might very well never come back. Ever. His uncle and aunt, too, might be… gone as well. He would never see any of them ever again.

Sunset of the second day, and no one else had arrived on the island. It was still just Michael, Tuesday, and Silvermin. Silvermin had taken his time exploring the island, and while he was excited to say that he had found a spring of drinkable (or at least, they *hoped* it was drinkable, especially considering the fact that they had all already drank quite a bit) freshwater, he also hadn't found any people or even that many animals—just a couple of birds that flew away when he approached, some tracks of some sort of hoofed animal, and a rat-like creature that had bitten his shoe.

"Tomorrow, we'll have a look along the beach. We should be able to find fish and perhaps a crab or two. The sea is bountiful, so we shouldn't have to eat only these fruits," Silvermin said, rather loudly. His voice jarred Michael out of his thoughts.

"How will we catch the fish?" Tuesday asked, eyes bright in the firelight.

"We could fashion some sort of net…" Silvermin scratched his chin thoughtfully. "Or we could herd the fish into the shallows and try to catch them with our hands."

"It might be a little hard catching fish with our *hands*, don't you think?" she asked flatly. "Let's try to be a little practical here…"

"Fine, Ms. Practical, why don't we use your skirt as a net?" Silvermin replied. Tuesday scowled at him and blushed, pulling her skirt down around her ankles.

"…Why don't we weave together leaves or stuff into a net?" Michael suggested. The fact that the other two had almost been arguing hadn't even crossed his mind. "I learned how to do that in school last year, and I think I could still do it."

"Oh, right! I learned that in school, too."

"I remember learning something similar when I was a boy. That sounds like a plan, then!"

Michael returned to watching the fire, completely unaware that he had broken up the first argument of the island.

"Did they argue often after that?" the psychologist asked. He'd been writing his notes throughout the story, trying to piece together the time on the island before it went south. Or before the rook came into play.

"…I can't really remember. I don't think so."

"Did you ever argue with either of them?"

"No. I didn't talk to them much, aside from planning."

The psychologist raised both eyebrows. "…Really." He ducked down behind his clipboard, scribbling furiously.

The third day was spent gathering palm tree leaves, tearing them into strips, and weaving them together. Silvermin turned out to be absolutely horrible at it, so he was delegated to gathering more materials and trying them in the water. Tuesday made a few atrocious ones before getting the hang of it, so she was allowed to stay working on them.

By noon, they had a fairly large pile of them and had run out of materials. "Aren't there any more?" Tuesday asked in confusion, looking back at the forest.

"Tropical forests aren't like normal forests, love. There aren't a lot of leaves of any sort on the ground," Silvermin replied briskly, looking down at the pile with his hands on his hips. "…As it is, this is probably more than enough. We can only use so many nets at a time."

"We can always use the rest of them," Michael pointed out, a little annoyed at the implication that their hard work was for naught. "You said so yourself—beds and fire and stuff."

"Why burn our hard work?" Tuesday scooted protectively in front of the pile. "We could make a roof, or some sort of shelter with them. I'd *love* to get out of this sun…"

The heat was starting to take its toll on all three of them. Michael had already sunburned his arms, being the only one without long sleeves, and they couldn't drink enough to satisfy their thirst. "Could we somehow use them for carrying water?"

"Why don't we just move to the spring?" she suggested. "We could tie a couple of them to trees for a bit of a roof, and the trees themselves will provide some shade as well. Plus we'll be right there for the water."

"What about the fire, then?" Silvermin asked in return. "We have to keep it going if we want anyone to know we're here. Plus, once we catch our food, we'll need to cook it. I don't suggest starting a fire in a forest."

Her face fell. She looked down at her feet, wiggling her toes in her sandals. "…Well then… I don't know."

"We could try to make a shelter out here. We'll just have to get our water whenever we're thirsty," Michael said quietly.

And so the rest of the day was spent trying to find materials to make a shelter. There were a couple of small trees they managed to pull out of the ground, but aside from that, there wasn't much they could do without an ax. Tuesday managed to create a bit of a lean-to, but it was a small one. Silvermin was the gentleman and let Tuesday and Michael have it.

Michael fell asleep to Silvermin staring at the fire, using Tuesday's shoulder as a pillow, listening to, "...And so Hamlet had to convince the world he was mad. Unfortunately, he seemed to go actually mad, partially due to the situations he was forced into, partially due to his family's problems..."

"How long were you on the island before the rook showed up?"

"He arrived on the fifth day. I think he was the one who started making things go badly for us. It was after we found him that we ran out of food."

"How?"

"We never could catch any fish, and there were only so many coconuts and bananas..." The patient's voice trailed off. The psychologist, for his part, couldn't decide if it was bitterly or regretfully. "We had been exploring the island and looking for more food... We didn't find any. We just found the rook."

Michael's stomach growled loudly. He wrapped his arms around his waist, trying to quiet it. He hadn't gotten to eat since yesterday afternoon, and that was just a sparse couple of coconuts shared with Tuesday and Silvermin.

The businessman was off on his own looking for food, insisting on doing so since he supposedly had a better grasp of the island. Tuesday was stuck with Michael and they were only allowed to search the forest near the beach. This made for very boring searching, since they had already combed the area several times in previous searches.

"...There are animal tracks, but I haven't seen any animals..." Tuesday murmured, gesturing vaguely down to some barely discernable prints in the sand. She wiped her brow and looked up at the sun overhead. Since they were still so close to the beach, the forest wasn't very dense, and the sun was merciless even in the sparse shade. "We're going to have to go back for water soon, huh?"

"Yeah," he replied automatically, swallowing thickly. Come to think of it, he was thirsty, too...

Tuesday sighed. "Let's go then."

The pair turned around. In front of them, perched on a crooked banana plant, sat a black bird. The bird calmly watched them, not at all alarmed that humans were just a sparse foot or two in front of it.

"What's a *crow* doing here?" Tuesday asked aloud. Michael shrugged—like he knew. The bird tilted its head, watching them with one black, beady eye. "They don't normally live on tropical islands... Do they?"

"I don't think so," he replied automatically. He *really* didn't know a thing about crows or tropical islands or where the subjects may or may not overlap. "It doesn't seem to be very scared of us."

"If we could catch it..."

The bird lowered its head, cawed, and then flew off. Tuesday sighed, running a hand through her bangs. Michael didn't feel any different from before; she was obviously disappointed. Why they would want to catch a crow, he didn't know. Unless they could eat it... His stomach growled again.

The two slowly made their way back towards the spring.

Water would help sate their hunger, if only for a little while. Plus, it was important to keep themselves hydrated, as Silvermin kept telling them.

Halfway there, however, they ran into the bird again. It was perched on a fern this time, the plant bowed nearly to the ground under its weight. The bird appeared to be smiling at them.

Tuesday hummed to herself happily and peeled off her sweater. She held it out like a net in front of herself, approaching the bird carefully. It made no move to fly away. Michael moved a bit so he could watch, however, and immediately the black bird's eyes were on him. Tuesday froze, poised to throw the sweater. The bird still made no move to leave, so she took a very cautious step forward. No response, so another followed.

Tuesday dove at the bird with her sweater. The crow flew out of the way with a caw—straight at Michael. He yelped and ducked, the bird missing his head by the tip of its feathers. It flew off into the forest once more, continuing its laugh-like call.

"Damn that bird!" Tuesday snarled, pushing herself back up onto her hands and knees. She blew some hair out of her eyes, shook her head, and got fully to her feet. "I was so close..."

"What's all the noise about?!" Michael and Tuesday both jumped when Silvermin came crashing through the foliage. He looked worried—actually, he looked downright distraught. Panting slightly, he looked over them both a couple times, then, satisfied that there were no obvious injuries, narrowed his eyes. "Why the bloody hell were you two shouting so loudly?"

"There was this bird—"

"There was a crow and it—"

They had started speaking at the same time. When they realized this, Tuesday and Michael looked at each other. Taking a deep breath, the teenage girl continued, "There was a crow and we were trying to catch it. I missed."

"And it tried to attack me!" Michael added angrily.

Silvermin looked between the pair. Then, he smiled ruefully. "…Really. A crow, on a tropical island? I don't doubt it was a bird, but—"

"I'm serious, it was a crow. Which way did it go?" Tuesday replied flatly. Michael pointed behind him, scowling in the direction the bird had flew off in. "Come on, we'll show you. It doesn't seem at all afraid of humans, and we've been able to get pretty close to it…"

"I'll believe it when I see it," Silvermin said under his breath, adjusting his shirt's collar.

Tuesday took Michael's hand as they led the businessman through the forest, on the lookout for the black bird. They found the spring first, though, and decided to stop for a break. Silvermin still *clearly* doubted the presence of a crow on the island, but the two younger ones stood their ground. They had definitely seen one.

Michael cupped his hands in the cool water and brought it to his mouth, not-so-accidentally spilling most of it down his shirtfront on the way. He caught Tuesday frowning at the wasteful action, but he really couldn't help it. It was so hot out, and he was already sunburned. The water felt too good to pass up, even if it meant disobeying her.

As he guiltily looked away, however, he found the bird again. It was perched on a rock not a foot from where they were sitting, watching them silently. "Look!" Even at his surprised shout, the bird didn't move a muscle. It really didn't seem scared of them at all.

"Eh?" Silvermin blinked a couple times and even rubbed his eyes. Tuesday shot him a triumphant look. He caught it and frowned, clearing his throat. "*Hate* to break it to you, love, but that's not a crow."

26

"What—?!"

"It's technically not a crow, no. It's a rook. It's too small to be a crow or a raven, so it's a rook by default. Not a crow." The brunette girl rolled her eyes at the technicality and opened her mouth to retort. The rook interrupted her, however, by flying directly in between her and Silvermin, leaving once more. "Bold bird…"

Michael stared after the departing rook, unable to figure out a single reason why it would be on the island. It obviously wasn't native, and it was the only one they'd come across. Was it lost, like they were? Or did it actually have a reason for being on the island?

The rest of the day, Michael alternated between wondering about the rook and what they were going to eat. They never did find any other food, or even any other animals for that matter. Silvermin complained about some impossible-to-track animal tracks, but that really only made matters worse. It made them think of the meal they could have had.

"We could try our hand at fishing again…"

"We've already tried. It just doesn't work."

Michael lay limply on the sand, hungry and exhausted. They had walked in circles the entire day, sometimes chasing the rook, sometimes doubling back to drink at the spring, but never finding anything but slightly dirty water to fill their stomachs with. He had suggested eating some of the plants that grew on the island, but Tuesday had shot him down, explaining that some plants were poisonous and they really didn't know which ones were safe to eat and which were not. A mistake could easily prove fatal.

"We could always go the route of *Lord of the Flies*," Tuesday joked. Michael didn't get the humor in her voice, but then again, he didn't know what *Lord of the Flies* was. Probably another book she had read. Was it like *Lord of the Rings*? Since he was lying down, he missed the oddly blank look Silvermin had given her. "We have a little boy here and everything."

"What's that?" Michael asked tiredly, eyelids drooping. It was only a little after sunset and still pretty bright out, but he was so tired lately…

"A book about a plane crash. A bunch of young boys, probably around your age, end up on an island by themselves and have to fend for themselves. It's a metaphor for civilization and how easily and quickly it can decline into little more than hysteria and chaos," she explained effortlessly.

Michael hadn't understood most of the last of it, but he understood the first part, at least. "…Then what do they do that *we* haven't tried yet? Besides the declining part."

Tuesday stayed uncharacteristically silent, especially considering he was asking her a book question. Michael raised his head up out of the sand, surprised to see her turn away from him. "Um… I didn't mean…"

"Cannibalism. They ended up eating another one of the boys," Silvermin replied in a flat tone, staring out at the ocean.

"Oh." Michael's head went back down into the sand. That probably wasn't something they should try.

The next day and the day after that, they didn't find any more food, however. The spring wasn't giving out as much water, either. Neither Tuesday nor Silvermin mentioned *Lord of the Flies* again. Michael tried not to think about it, too, but it was hard to not think when all they had to do *was* think.

So soon after losing both parents, he really didn't think he should be thinking about the prospect of killing—and eating!—another human being. It would mean that there would only be two left on the island, only two survivors of the shipwreck. And what if no rescue came after that? Would one of the remaining two be eaten? And what would happen to that last person, then?

...And there was, of course, the matter of *who* it would be. The thought of killing animals made him a little bit squeamish, but as they actually hadn't caught anything, he really hadn't had to confront that problem. Killing a person, however, that was entirely different. Both Tuesday and Silvermin had faces, personalities, *names*, lives. They were humans. Humans just didn't *eat* other humans.

Michael's stomach growled, begging for food. He laid a hand over it, resting in the shade of their lean-to, and tried to ignore his body's plea.

People didn't eat other people. It really was as simple as that. Oh, if only they could find that rook again, or that hoofed animal Silvermin kept mentioning, or really anything. He'd gladly eat coconuts or bananas at that point. It seemed as if they'd eaten so well on that second day, but now it seemed so distant and just a fond memory.

Day eight—or was it nine?—dawned bright and cheery and hungrily. Michael's stomach *demanded* food, loudly and rather angrily. He groaned and rolled over onto Tuesday's arm, nestling into her shoulder. She mumbled something and put her free arm around him, pulling him closer to her in her sleep. Michael squeezed his eyes shut tightly and tried to focus on breathing instead of his constant hunger or thirst. He inhaled and exhaled, but that only made his stomach growl more, so he paid attention to Tuesday in front of him instead.

Her mascara was smudged all over her eyes, giving them a dark, almost raccoon-like look, her hair was tousled all over the place, her skirt was torn and her sweater was dirty, but she told him stories and always had a smile or an answer to his questions. Michael sighed, drifting back to sleep, concentrating on her.

When he awoke again, she was crawling out of the lean-to.

He rubbed his eyes sleepily, trying to get the sand out of them. The problem with living so long on an island was that sand got *everywhere*. He yawned, ignored his stomach, and pushed himself up onto his elbows.

Outside the lean-to, Silvermin and Tuesday were talking in hushed tones. Michael lay back down on his stomach, swallowing to try to wet his dry mouth. He could barely hear more than a murmur from them. His hunger wouldn't let him go back to sleep this time, however, so he tried to listen to them to wake himself up.

Tuesday was talking in that worried tone she got when she was wringing her hands. "Mr. Silvermin, you are a grown man and can last longer than we can. We're just children. We need food. I don't know what we're going to do, but we're going to have to do *something*."

"What do you propose on doing, hmm? If you haven't noticed, we can't do much right now. We can keep the fire burning to attract any attention in the area, but until we get rescued, we can't do much!" He sounded annoyed, and his words had a rehearsed sound to them, as if he didn't personally believe himself. Maybe they had had the argument before.

"We have to stop rationing the water. It's all we have. It'll run out eventually, anyway…" She trailed off, mumbled something too quiet to hear, and then raised her voice again. "We've just been assuming rescue will come…"

"It will. A whole ship goes down? They're on their way here," Silvermin replied firmly. Much too forcefully for it to be reassuring.

"We have to find a way to survive until then." Tuesday's words had taken on the same weight that his had. They were not trying to talk to each other; they were talking to themselves, trying to convince themselves of things. Michael wasn't exactly sure what, though, since he was still a little drowsy and much too naïve about the world to understand the choices they were trying to make. "We have to," she repeated.

The psychologist swallowed, a little unnerved by the way this story was turning out. Oh, sure, he had seen dozens of truly disturbing things in his patients, but very rarely did one affect him this much. Too much had happened in too little time to this patient, and it was obvious the result.

"Tell me... What sort of effect did the rook have on you all?" he asked. The bird hadn't seemed to play a very large part, but then again, the horror had only started.

The patient's head lolled to the side as there was much thought about how to respond. "...I don't know about the others... But I had a nightmare about him that night."

"Oh? Why don't you tell me what it was like?"

"Terrible."

After another day with no food and nothing in his stomach save water and a bit of sand he had tried eating, Michael slept fitfully. He couldn't get comfortable. Tuesday, however, slept like the dead, arms outstretched from where he had rolled out of them.

Eventually, and not wanting to wake her, he crawled out of the lean-to. The fire was crackling somewhat weakly, not much more than a couple of pathetic flames and embers. Silvermin was curled up beside it, asleep, using his jacket as a pillow.

Michael rubbed at his eyes and yawned, wondering about getting a drink of water. If he got one, would the other two be mad at him? ...Would they ever find out?

31

He yawned again and got shakily to his feet. He hadn't been feeling so well lately—pretty weak and he got dizzy—but he chalked it up to being hungry. The boy padded silently out of the light of the fire and made it all the way to the edge of the trees before he felt someone watching him. Guiltily, he turned around, but Silvermin was still asleep by the fire. Michael, confused, squinted into the darkness. It looked like Tuesday was still sleeping, too, or at the very least she hadn't come out of the lean-to.

Michael felt the hairs on the back of his neck rise. The feeling of being watched persisted; who was out there? Was it an animal of some sort? Or was it a person? He had never been into scary stories very much, but he couldn't help but recall a couple he'd heard about various monsters and psychos stalking people and killing them...

He continued to look about him carefully, watching the darkness for any signs of movement. Between the ocean's waves and his overly loud breathing, he couldn't hear anything. The psycho could come up right behind him and he wouldn't even hear him. Just to be sure, Michael looked over his shoulder. Nothing there, thankfully. He backed up until his outstretched arm touched a tree and hastily slid up to it. Maybe he wasn't so thirsty after all... But he made it all the way to the forest, so why not try to go the rest of the way?

Michael circled around the tree, keeping his back pressed against the rough bark. He still didn't hear anything save his heart thundering in his ribcage, or see anything save the blackness of the night. He was dimly aware of the fact that he was only working himself up more.

He reached out his hand for the next tree and scampered over to it when he found it a bit too far for him to touch. And so he continued winding his way through the forest, tree by tree, steadily getting calmer when nothing jumped out with a knife. He made it all the way to the spring, in fact, before he found what had been watching him.

The rook sat on one of the rocks, watching him with bright eyes. Michael pressed a hand to his wildly beating heart when he caught sight of the bird. He had been expecting something, yes, but not *actually* expecting something to be there... "Thank God it's just you..." he whispered, voice hoarse and shaky.

Michael ignored the bird and leaned down to take a drink. He made up his mind to not drink that much, just enough to take the edge off his hunger and thirst.

"Have you decided on a course to take yet?"

Michael coughed, nearly choking on the water. His head snapped up to stare, wide-eyed, at the rook. Had it just *spoken*? If not—who had?! "Wh-What are you talking about? Who said that?!"

The rook tilted its head to one side jerkily, beak glinting in the faint moonlight. "I asked you a question. Don't answer me with two more. It's very counterproductive," it replied.

Michael nearly fainted. He slowly edged away, suddenly not thirsty at all. He couldn't believe they'd nearly caught the bird to eat earlier—is that why it was here? To get revenge or something against them for wanting to eat it? "I-I-I—"

"Oh, aren't you articulate," the rook said, beak clicking on the last syllable. It tilted its head to the other side, regarding him with one eye. "...It's obvious you haven't made up your mind yet. I'll have to come back later for the answer."

With that, the rook cawed loudly. Michael bolted upright, soaked in a cold sweat. He hit his head on top of the lean-to, however, and several of the palm leaves fell on top of both himself and Tuesday. She awoke in confusion, wiping leaves out of her hair as she squinted up at him. "What's going on...?" she asked, blinking in the darkness.

"I…" Michael pressed his hands to his cheeks. Had it just been a dream, then? It seemed so. He was still in their bed, at any rate, and the horizon out the side of the lean-to was beginning to show some pinkish light. It wasn't the middle of the night, so it *must* have been a dream—or nightmare, really.

"Are you alright?" Now more awake, Tuesday sat up as well, frowning worriedly. Without waiting for an answer, she pulled him into a hug, running her fingers through his blond hair soothingly. "It's okay… Want to go back to sleep?"

Not really; he was wide awake now. "No, I'm not tired," he whispered, closing his eyes.

"Then let's get up. …Who knows, maybe some animals will be awake this early. Maybe we'll be able to get some food today," she replied in a sigh, continuing playing with his hair, making no move to get up. Michael didn't necessarily mind. Now he was comfortable, and maybe even perhaps a little sleepy. Just as he was thinking that, however, Tuesday released him and got to her feet, dusting off her skirt as she did so. He scrambled after her and stood with her, looking at the partially wrecked lean-to. "This shouldn't take too long to fix. We can do it later. Let's go get a bit of water and then we can see if we can't find any food today, shall we?" she asked brightly, taking his hand and marching off towards the forest.

Michael shivered, remembering his nightmare. It was already fading with the night, but he distinctly remembered the rook and its condescending, vaguely frightening tone. He concentrated on telling himself it was just a dream, only a dream, it wasn't real. The technique worked, for they were at the spring before he had the chance to wonder what he might do if the rook was still there. The bird was nowhere in sight.

He let out a breath he hadn't known he was holding.

They found yet more taunting tracks, but they found no animals whatsoever. Not even any birds, rook included. When they returned to their camp, Silvermin was awake and tending the fire. He stood up when they got near. "Where have you two been?!" he demanded.

"We were just getting a bit of water and looked for food," Tuesday replied hesitantly, gripping Michael's hand tightly. "We weren't gone long and we didn't want to wake you, anyway."

"I'm not sleep-deprived. You should tell me whenever you leave the beach." He still seemed angry, but he was rapidly losing that anger. Michael realized that he had been worried about them.

"We'll tell you next time," he said softly, interrupting Tuesday's retort. She looked down at him, and then over at the man, relaxing. She let go of Michael's hand. "We promise. Right?"

"Right," she replied with a slightly forced smile.

Silvermin sighed and sat back down near the fire. He hung his head, but immediately it came back up as he surveyed the pair. He seemed to be thinking about something. Michael found this a little disconcerting, since the businessman had always been open with them. He seemed to feel responsible for them and was always watching out for them. For him to not share something with them... It seemed off.

Michael and Tuesday set about to fixing their shelter while Silvermin went off to search for food, yet again. They knew it would be a futile endeavor, but it wouldn't hurt to hope, right? And regardless of the actual possibility of finding food, they had that small, hungry hope growing inside them.

Once Silvermin was out of earshot, Tuesday gave Michael a one-armed hug as she lifted up part of the roof. "You're such a little angel. You're too cute and too nice," she said with a chuckle. Michael smiled, feeling pleased with the compliment.

Silvermin came back late—it was almost sunset—with empty hands. He had tried tracking any animals he saw or spotted any sort of trail, but to no avail. All three of them sat around the fire, stomachs complaining loudly, and stared at the flames. No one knew what to say. They were getting hungrier and hungrier, and more and more often Michael got his dizzy spells. Sooner or later, one of them would pass out, and that would mean that they were in serious trouble.

…As if they weren't already.

Silvermin sat completely still, whereas Tuesday wouldn't stop fidgeting. Michael was lost in his own little world. This time, the fire wasn't the one mesmerizing him, however. He was thinking—about what would happen to them. They were all so hungry, and each day, it was visible how much weaker they were getting. Their water supply wasn't going to last forever, either, even he knew that. With no food and eventually no water… They wouldn't last. They would *die*.

Michael pulled his knees to his chest and buried his face in them. They would all die. They would be gone, like his parents and aunt and uncle and everyone else on board that ship. People might never find their bodies. They would just lie on the sand for forever, maybe even becoming food for that rook. That would be irony; they would die of starvation, but their bodies would be used for food. Dead humans equaled food. Funny how that worked out.

Michael felt his thoughts starting to drift towards the cannibalism the other two had mentioned before.

"…I'm so hungry." Tuesday's voice drew the attention of both males. She sounded nearly ready to cry. Eyes bright in the firelight, she stared listlessly at the flames and spoke again, "I'm so hungry… What will we do? We'll die at this rate."

36

"I know, love," Silvermin replied quietly. Michael looked at him, if only to look away from Tuesday's almost-crying face, and was surprised to see the man look so sad. He wasn't ready to cry, not like her, but he seemed like he had just heard something terribly tragic. Like something major had just happened and he couldn't have stopped it.

"We have to *do* something," Tuesday pleaded, tears running down her cheeks now. Michael's stomach grumbled and he wrapped his arms around himself, closing his eyes.

"Tomorrow. If we don't find food tomorrow…" Silvermin trailed off with a cough. "We will talk about this tomorrow more seriously. If we don't find food."

Michael didn't know what he was really talking about, but he knew that it made him feel cold and nervous. He fell asleep with in Tuesday's arms, as usual, that night. She didn't tell him a story, however, and instead held him close and kissed the top of his head. "I'm so sorry, little angel." Her voice was so soft, he wasn't sure he'd heard her, or if she had even spoken at all.

And so Michael fell asleep.

They didn't find any food the next day.

The three of them had searched the entire island up and down, so desperate it hurt. Michael didn't know why, but it was contagious, and he nearly broke down in tears when he came to the northernmost edge of the island while seeing absolutely *nothing*. They couldn't find any food. What would they do now?

He swore at one point that he saw that rook, but he only got a glimpse, so he couldn't be sure. At any rate, they couldn't catch the bird, so they couldn't use it for food.

That afternoon, the three came back together with empty hands and even emptier stomachs. Michael noticed that Tuesday's sweater was a bit baggier on her than it had been originally. Silvermin's shirt hung more loosely on his shoulders.

They were officially starving.

"...We didn't find any food," Michael said shamefully, hanging his head. "None on the whole island."

"What are we going to do now...?" Tuesday asked, looking up at the businessman through her bangs. Her mascara-smudged eyes brimmed with tears.

Silvermin took a deep breath, then exhaled. "We are going to draw lots."

He seemed to already have a plan as to how to go about such a thing. They took a palm leave and cut it into strips, then cut those strips into ones of varying lengths. Michael didn't dare ask what they were doing this for; he had a very, *very* bad feeling about it and was operating under the rather naïve principle that if he didn't acknowledge the problem, it would go away. They dug a narrow, deep hole and dumped the makeshift straws into the hole.

"We are going to draw three each. There will be more than enough for each of us," Silvermin explained, voice hollow. He wouldn't look at either of them and was instead staring fiercely at the hole at his feet. "The one who has the shortest combined length loses."

No one asked what would be lost.

"Close your eyes, and reach in. Just grab whichever one is there—don't go fishing around for it."

The three of them knelt down around the hole, and one by one, started picking up their palm lots. He drew first and picked out a medium-length one. Or, at least, he assumed it was medium length. And it was, at least compared to Tuesday's—hers was long—and Silvermin's—his was short. The two older ones exchanged a look. Tuesday then turned to Michael with a shaky, watery smile, and asked him if he would draw his second one.

The pressure mounted, and Michael still wasn't exactly

sure why, which really only made it worse. He was sweating when he reached into the hole a second time, and drew out a fairly short one. That wasn't good. He glanced at Tuesday as she drew out a medium-length one; she had two pretty long ones. Silvermin drew out a long one, which balanced out his short one. Who was winning? Michael looked down at the two clutched tightly in his hand. Was he losing?

Tuesday looked at him expectantly, wanting him to draw another. Michael shook his head and squeezed his eyes shut. "I-I don't want to draw another…"

"But—"

"I'll draw," Silvermin said gruffly, reaching in for his third. He drew out another long one. He looked to Tuesday, who mutely took her turn as next. Michael watched as she took one out, a pretty short one. Michael swallowed; he couldn't stall any longer. He had to draw his final straw.

Michael kept his eyes closed when he reached in, and didn't open them until he pulled out one of the strips. He finally cracked open one eye, and was immensely relieved to see that it was a long one. But… Silvermin had two long ones and a short one, and Tuesday had a long one, a medium one, and a short one. Michael had one of each, too.

"We're going to have to measure," Silvermin said in that same hollow voice. He laid down his three strips in a line so that they touched, creating a long straw. Michael crawled over and laid his down as well. His was about three inches shorter than Silvermin's. His heart jumped into his throat and he found it suddenly very hard to breathe.

"Mine's shorter…"

Before he could finish that thought, Tuesday laid hers down. The line was nearly even to Michael's—but… just a little shorter. Barely half an inch shorter. Michael and Tuesday stared at these results, neither of them breathing.

"…That's it, then," Silvermin said flatly. His voice was still empty. He seemed a little shocked by the results, though. "So… We'll… discuss the details then, love?"

Tuesday continued staring down at the shortest line. She didn't reply.

Michael wanted to nudge her, or say something, or even hug her, but he didn't do any of them. He didn't know why not. He could only concentrate on the fact that he had the middle length. He hadn't lost. But what had Tuesday lost?

Silvermin reached out and touched her on the shoulder. It was a light touch, barely brushing against her sweater's fabric. She jumped as though burned, however, head snapping up. Her eyes were dry, wide, staring, staring blindly ahead. "I… I lost," she said blankly. Michael nearly flinched; her hollow voice was much worse than Silvermin's.

"Let's talk about this, love," Silvermin said quietly, trying to sound… something. Michael really wasn't sure what he was aiming for, but it made him sound like he was far away. "We can talk about this, how we'll go about this. Let's not make this tougher than it has to be."

Tuesday opened her mouth to reply—and caught sight of Michael, who had been looking at her. She immediately closed it again, rubbed her eye with her palm—smudging her makeup even further—and smiled warmly. "…Yeah."

CHAPTER THREE

Blessed Is He Who **Suffers Temptation**

Michael was told to go to bed. He silently went to the lean-to and listened to Silvermin lead Tuesday away. He could still hear them talking over the ocean, but he couldn't make out any of their words.

He wasn't sure he wanted to.

Michael kept his eyes shut tight and tried to keep his mind shut, too. He couldn't help but think, though. He thought he had a feeling as to what they were talking about, but he dreaded ever finding out if he was right or not. He really, honestly didn't want to know. He just wanted to wake up, to find out that this was all a bad dream. His parents would still be with him, they wouldn't be on this horrible island, Tuesday wouldn't have those dark eyes or that look, and Silvermin wouldn't have to sound so empty.

Michael didn't hear the footsteps until something nudged the top of his head. Eyes wide open now, he shakily got to his hands and knees and raised his head. Had they come to a decision? What were they talking about, anyway? What had Tuesday lost?

He didn't find Tuesday returning, or Silvermin checking up on him. The boy found himself looking up into a skull, however. His breath caught.

It wasn't a human skull, but that didn't make the shock any less heart stopping. The eyes were merely darkened sockets; he could still feel its gaze. The skull was missing a bottom jaw and its snout was sharp and partially broken, splintered and cracked. Two dark, curving horns protruded from the back of the skull. Michael belatedly realized it was a ram's skull when he forced himself to inhale.

He stared at the skull, shivering. It remained motionless, staring at him. Michael slowly backed up until he was sitting on his knees, shaking hands held defensively in front of him. What *was* that thing?

The skull suddenly dipped lower, and Michael's heart nearly stopped again. He realized with that jolt that it was connected to a *body*, and the skull was supposed to be the body's *head*. Behind the head and below it, he could only see shaggy, black fur, blending in with the dark night around it.

"You've come to a decision." When the thing spoke, Michael backed up until he fell over, chest heaving and eyes wide. The skull jerkily moved to the side. It was as if the creature tilted its head. It took a step forward, and blue eyes darted down to find claws stepping into the lean-to.

Michael screamed.

The thing patiently waited for him to stop screaming. The boy's voice finally gave out and he resorted to backing up again and whimpering. Neither Tuesday nor Silvermin came running up, unfortunately, which meant Michael was alone with the skull monster. It jerkily stepped forward, ducking its head to enter the lean-to. It seemed to walk on four legs, and its front two ended in viciously sharp claws, almost talon-like.

"Don't do that again," the thing commanded. Michael swallowed. He didn't even consider not listening to it. It took another step forward, crouching down to let two monstrously large folded wings into the lean-to as well. Michael was nearly on his back, staring up at it as it loomed over him with its empty eye sockets and splintered jaw.

Michael couldn't reply to it. He was too terrified to now, after his initial, futile scream. His throat felt as if it had closed up and he could do nothing more than offer a faint wheeze.

The creature leaned down until its skull was mere inches from his face. Michael could tell that it wasn't breathing. "You've come to a decision. Is it one you're happy with? Will you be able to be happy with it at the end of your life?"

Michael opened his mouth, but again, no sound would come out. It tilted its head to the side again, and he could have sworn it was smiling at him, as if it knew his plight. "I—What a-are you?" Suddenly, he could speak. Michael tried not to think about how he had the feeling that the creature had *allowed* him to speak. He didn't want it to have that much power over him.

"I am the Rook." It leaned down and touched the tip of its jaw to Michael's forehead.

The boy bolted upright, chest heaving and cold sweat trickling uncomfortably down his neck. Tuesday was sitting near the edge of the lean-to. She jumped and stared at him in alarm at the sudden movement. Michael suppressed a relieved sob that it was just a dream and rubbed his eyes, trying to wipe away the tears. He felt like he'd just lost something terribly important to him, but he had no idea what it might have been. That somehow made it worse.

Tuesday didn't ask what was wrong. Instead, she exhaled slowly and placed a hand on his leg. Michael looked down at her hand, the bracelet shining faintly from the firelight. He was completely unused to seeing her so... empty. Hollow. She normally had a smile or a hug for him, but she had never looked so *broken* before. Michael leaned forward and put his hand over hers, staring hard up at her. Tuesday just looked down at the gesture.

"...You're such an angel. Thank you." She still wasn't smiling. She took her hand out from under his and used it to wipe at her eyes. She then half-turned away from him, staring out into the night, twirling her bracelet for something to do with her hands. Michael, heart still pounding in his chest from his nightmare, crawled forward and sat down beside her.

"What's wrong?" he asked quietly.

"I..." She paused, searching for the right words. "Tomorrow, we're... You'll be strong for me, right?"

Michael wasn't expecting that. "Of course," he replied in confusion. Why did he have to be strong for her? He had a suspicion he knew what it was, but he would not acknowledge the dark little thought. He would never acknowledge it.

Tuesday sniffed and rubbed at her eyes again. She had been weepy lately, but she was more subdued now. Like she had run out of actual tears to cry. "Good."

Michael, on the other hand, still had plenty of tears to spend. He scooted closer to her and wrapped one arm around her waist, leaning his head on her shoulder. "...Don't be sad," he told her, unsure of what else to say. He really didn't want to ask what was wrong; he didn't want to know the answer. The dark little thought reared its ugly head once more.

Tuesday laughed. It wasn't a happy laugh, though. It was more of a sad, or angry, or bitter laugh—it could have been a lot of things, but not a happy laugh. "I-I was going to get married, you know." He didn't know where that subject had come from or why she was telling him. He only listened, however. "I mean, I don't have th-the ring, but we had talked about it, and we were going to... He gave me this."

She held up her arm, the silver bracelet sliding down on her wrist, charms swinging from the movement.

"He's been so patient with m-me, and he's so sw-sweet...! H-His name is Chris an-an-and I love him *so much*!" With that, she broke down, and Michael found out that she wasn't out of tears, after all. She kept talking through her crying, most of it incoherent whimpering and sobbing, Michael knew, at that point, what she and Silvermin had been talking about and couldn't ignore the point any longer.

What seemed like hours later, Tuesday had cried herself to

sleep. The remains of her mascara had run down her cheeks, giving her two black lines running straight down to the bottom of her jaw. Michael wanted to wipe it off, but he was worried he'd wake her, and he thought she should be able to sleep.

Michael shakily sighed and pressed the heels of his palms against his eyes. His parents had left him. Now Tuesday was leaving him. This island was going to rip everything from him until it eventually killed him, too—he knew that much. He didn't see any way out of it, really, since you couldn't fight against an *island* and the ocean was just as fierce and killed just as many and in the end everyone would die anyway—

He jerked his hands away from his eyes, interrupting his gradually crashing train of thought, when he heard a noise.

The ram skull with the empty eyes and black body was staring at him. The Rook was staring at him.

Michael couldn't even scream this time. He knew it had to be a dream, a nightmare, it *had* to be, but it didn't make it any less terrifying. Worse still, he could see the thing's body in the firelight now. It had an emaciated, starved look—legs too skinny, ribcage standing out in such sharp contrast compared to its stomach, looking like not much more than its odd, glossy fur and bones.

It probably wasn't.

"Do you feel sorry for her?" the Rook asked mildly. Michael instinctively looked back at its head and regretted it immediately, averting his eyes once more.

"Yes," he replied. Why did it even need to *ask*?

"Why?"

"She's going to die."

"I'm aware of that. I've come to take her away."

Michael snuck a glance up at the skull. It was still in the same position, sightlessly staring at him out of its empty eye sockets. "…A-Are you the Grim Reaper?" That's who he had always assumed took dead people away, unless it was God—but really, the monster before him could *not* be God or any of His angels, so he supposed it really couldn't be anything *but* the Grim Reaper.

"Oh, no. You couldn't pay me to take that job," the Rook replied, the barest hint of amusement evident in its voice. Michael frowned in confusion. "I've merely come to take her away. Kill her, really. I won't be the one to kill her physical body, at least not in the technical sense, but I'll kill her and take her away all the same."

It didn't sound the least bit remorseful, either. Michael's frown hardened into a scowl. "Why are you doing it, then? If it's not your job—why would you want to kill anybody?!" he demanded, glaring at the skull.

"Why?" it repeated, seemingly taken aback by the question.

"Yes, why! Don't you have any sort of regret or feelings or heart?!"

"Don't raise your voice to me." Michael ducked his head down and quieted, though he was still silently fuming. So this thing was going to kill Tuesday and apparently didn't have a reason for doing so. How could that be? Even if that were true… Well, if it wasn't set in stone, he was going to fight. "Don't even think about it. *You* were the ones who decided to kill one of your own in the first place," it added, tilting its head again with a sharp twitch to the right. Its jerky movements were at odds with its smooth voice.

"But—"

"Don't bother arguing." The Rook moved its head again so that it was vertical once more. "I've already made up my mind, anyway."

"…But *why*?" He had to know. He had to know why it felt

47

the need to take Tuesday away, to *kill* her.

"Because I *want* to."

"Why do you want to, then?"

The Rook seemed to contemplate the more specific question. After an agonizingly long pause, it said simply, "Because it will hurt you."

Michael had no idea what to say to that. He had never met anyone—or anything—so spiteful before, anything that would kill others solely to hurt him. The fact that any creature could have that much hatred and violence in its heart was something he couldn't fully comprehend. The fact that it was more than willing to exercise that cruelty was even more appalling.

"Besides," the Rook said, taking a step closer and looming over him like it had just hours before, "Now you don't have anyone left. I don't have to compete with anyone else for your attention."

"Y-You could have just asked, I would have—"

"Come now, Michael, let's not be stupid. Would you have *really* spent any time at all with me if you had anyone else in the world to spend time with? I would not be the first you'd run to in any situation. I can tell even now that you're absolutely terrified of me." There was definite amusement in its voice now, but it somehow still retained the tone of talking down to a misbehaving child.

He stared up at the Rook, scarcely daring to breathe. He half-expected it to continue speaking; it had sounded so desperate to talk and had almost *babbled* with the way it prattled on. Still, as the thing was silent and seemed to want Michael to acknowledge it somehow, he croaked out, "I am. I *am* terrified of you—"

And that was all it needed from Michael.

"Very good! As well you should be!" the Rook crowed,

bobbing its skull head. "Never lose that. Even if you hate me as well, never lose your fear, understand? Just remember that I am the cause for everything. Everything you've lost, every misfortune you have suffered and *will* suffer, it's all because I *wanted* them to happen. Remember that, and we will get along *swimmingly*."

This was getting to be too much. Michael tore his gaze away from the monster before him, staring instead at the fire. It had come to him in another nightmare and said it was killing everyone he ever loved or cared about or *knew* and it was really only trying to get a rise out of him, or *something*. He closed his eyes and took a deep breath, trying to calm himself down. He was intensely aware of the Rook's non-existent eyes on him, however. Michael tried telling himself it was a dream, just a dream, only a dream...

"You're thinking this is another one of your human nightmares, correct?" the Rook asked curiously, jarring him out of his self-consolation. Michael cracked one eye open and nodded warily. Maybe closing his eyes around it wasn't the best of ideas.

Then the Rook laughed.

Michael snapped both eyes open and stared at it. He knew it was laughter only because it would be the only response possible from the monster, but it hardly sounded anything like it. It was rough and hoarse and reminded him of sandpaper and people screaming. And here he thought he could possibly get any more scared.

"This isn't a dream," the Rook told him, cutting off its laughter abruptly.

"Y-You can't lie to me, I *know* it is." Michael didn't like how his voice shook, but at least he was able to string together a coherent sentence this time without an interruption.

"Really." It wasn't a question. The Rook then, with erratic, jerking movements, stood up on its hind legs. Michael reeled back, especially as its claws caught the firelight. It stretched its wings for a brief second before folding them around itself. The black feathers slowly melded together until the Rook was standing in a black cloak, with only its ram skull head visible above it.

The Rook leaned down and grabbed Michael by the hair, forcing his head back. Tears immediately sprang to his eyes from both the shock of the pain and the pain itself. "Does this still feel like a dream?!" it demanded harshly, pulling.

"N-No—!"

"Good!" The Rook adjusted its claws so that they were digging into his scalp. He dragged the boy upright before stooping down again to grab Tuesday by the arm. Michael was yanked back up again when the Rook stood up fully. Tuesday didn't stir. The blond boy stared fearfully at her, trying to figure out if she was still breathing or not—but then, the Rook dug its claws even deeper into the top of his head. Michael grit his teeth and tried not to scream, ignoring the sensation that felt terrifyingly like blood trickling down his forehead.

Then the Rook was speaking again. "Since you are *aware* this is not a *dream*, we can continue on with the important things! Like how you are going to *believe me* when I say I am going to take every damn thing in the world away from you! Including her!"

"Wait, no—!"

"Don't talk back to me," the monster snarled, shoving its claws in deeper. "Don't you ever talk back to me again. Is this understood?"

Michael tried his best to nod, but the Rook's grip made it impossible. "Yes," he bit out.

The Rook unexpectedly threw both of them to the sand. Michael was immediately trying to stagger back up, one hand holding his head while the other reached out for Tuesday. The Rook crouched over her, fiddling with the sleeve of her sweater.

"Stop—" Michael realized too late that he had talked back again. His reflexes kicked in and he took a step back, arms now held defensively in front of him, waiting for more abuse. The Rook merely threw something at him before standing up once more.

"Keep it. It'll be all you have to remember her by—oh, *wait*, it won't, will it? Because you will get to *eat* tomorrow!" the Rook exclaimed in delight, grin clear in its voice. Michael looked down at his feet, where the thing the Rook had thrown lay. It was a silver charm bracelet, Tuesday's silver charm bracelet.

With trembling hands, Michael bent down and picked it up. "N-No, I don't want that, I don't want her to d-die. I don't." He addressed the bracelet in his hand rather than the monster holding Tuesday in front of him. Why was this all happening? Was it really all the fault of the Rook?

"…That's too bad," it replied unsympathetically. "Because she's going to die. You were the ones who decided to kill her, and you're going to be the ones who do it to her."

"If we hadn't decided that, would you still be here to take her away?" he asked in a small voice, afraid of the answer. He desperately hoped it would be a 'no', but knowing the Rook, even as little as he knew about it, it would say 'yes'. Even if it was a lie.

"Oh yes. Haven't you been listening, Michael? I'll take away *everything*." It thrust Tuesday forward, holding her upward under the arms. Her head lolled limply to one side. "Now say goodbye to her, Michael. This will be the last time you see her; don't you want to bid her farewell?"

"Don't say that!" Michael snapped, past the point of caring what the Rook did. It had already taken away his parents, his only family, his way home, and all those people on the ship, and now it was going to be taking away one of the last people in the world Michael could say he cared about. Even if he died from it, he wasn't going down without a fight. Not anymore.

The Rook seemed to sense this. It tilted its skull head to one side, the bottom of one horn brushing against its shoulder. "...You and I will get along magnificently."

Michael staggered forward, to do what he had no idea, but he never made it. Blackness overtook him.

And when he woke up again, the sun was shining brightly in the morning sky, Tuesday was gone, and a silver charm bracelet was hanging from his wrist.

The psychologist had given up on taking notes. He doubted he could get this story out of his mind, even if he'd wanted to. He also highly suspected it would be quite awhile before he would be able to sleep normally once more.

The patient across the table from him stared balefully at him, dark eyes daring him to say something.

He was never one to turn down a challenge, and moreover, it was his job to figure out what had really happened. "So... The Rook was the one who, er, killed Tuesday?"

"...In a way." The sentence was terse.

"Then what really happened?"

"We... I... I woke up, and..." The patient was now looking from side to side, grasping at straws. Trying to form a coherent answer. The psychologist leaned forward slightly, an unconscious movement to try to get closer to the truth. "W-We had decided to do that... You know... And we—we needed food, we were so hungry—so hungry, starving, dying, we were so hungry with our stomachs always growling and losing weight and never finding any food and we were desperate and tired and we couldn't do anything else we were so hungry we had to do something—"

"Please calm down!" The patient was losing grip again. The psychologist had realized early on that that tended to happen when confronting the nastier of the memories. And while the rambling told much about what had happened on that island, it was barely understandable and more often than not, the patient was stuck on a broken record loop, repeating the same things over and over while trying to mentally come to terms with it. The psychologist had run into cases with that problem in the past, but it was never easy to work with. "Take a deep breath and tell me what happened."

"We were so *hungry* and we couldn't think of anything else we were hungry we had to do something—"

"No, tell me what happened," he interrupted once more, adjusting his glasses. "Just the facts, please. You don't have to tell me what you were feeling." It was a cold statement, but a necessary one. Plus, what most patients didn't realize that the *way* they said something was usually more important than *what* they said. Even if he was going to get this information by tearing the most traumatic moment of his patient's life out by force, he would get it, and he would figure out how to help after that. One could only be fixed after they were broken, after all.

His patient looked down at the silver charm bracelet on that oh so thin wrist. It was absently tugged at, the dark, blank eyes above it looking blankly from side to side again. "...We were hungry, so we found a solution to it. We solved our hunger problem because we *needed* to, because we were so hungry, and so we did the only thing that we could." The words were starting to run on again, but there was a clear and conscious effort not to. The psychologist took notes. "We—We made straws and we drew them and the one with the shortest one was picked they lost and that way it was fair because none of us was any *better* than the others not really and we were trying so hard to be fair—"

"Please, Michael. Just tell me what happened."

"We drew straws and one of us came up short. It was fate. It had to be, right? The Rook was only the—the messenger or something like that he was only part of it, right? She suggested it, so that's why she died, right? Was she wrong for that?"

"Just tell me what happened." He couldn't answer that question, not without either forfeiting his decency or making the situation much, much worse. "…Tuesday drew the shortest straw, didn't she?" he prompted, as much of a lead as he could give.

"Yes. She did," came the flat reply.

"What happened to her?"

His patient finally looked up at him. "We killed her. We killed her and ate her."

CHAPTER FOUR

As We Stand With Our Backs **To Each Other**

One week later, just as Michael's stomach was starting to growl again and Silvermin was starting to look uncomfortable, rescue came.

During that week, the Rook was always uncomfortably close to him. Never when Silvermin was around, though, and Michael tried his best to hang around the man as often as he could because of that, but Silvermin often wandered off into the forest to be on his own. He said he was thinking; he did that quite a bit during that week.

The Rook was nowhere to be seen on the day that the helicopter finally found them. Michael was glad for it, though it made him nervous. He was constantly waiting for it to reappear.

He and Silvermin were rushed to a hospital and were asked to answer a lot of questions and give a lot of explanations. Michael kept his mouth firmly shut, even after he and Silvermin were separated. Both of them were malnourished and dehydrated. Michael didn't doubt that, but he still didn't appreciate it very much when they stuck him with all sorts of needles and ran dozens of tests.

The first night after their rescue, Michael was starting to doze off. It had been a long day. He'd nearly jumped out of his skin when he had first heard the helicopter, expecting the Rook but instead getting whisked back to civilization. Silvermin had told him to be quiet, and that was the last thing he had said to him; that made Michael infinitely more nervous. He knew what they had done was a bad thing—a very, *very* horrible thing. He didn't know what would happen to them now that they were in the company of people who would judge them for it, though. So he kept silent.

"Enjoying the nutrition?" Michael cracked open one eye to

see the ram skull nosing the IV bag. "It doesn't taste *nearly* as good as she did, though, does it?"

"Sh-Shut up..." he muttered, turning his head away from it. He was smacked on the shoulder rather roughly for the talking back. The one good thing about having to spend that last week haunted by the Rook was that he was learning that there was a line. As long as he didn't cross it, the Rook normally left him alone and unharmed.

Well, alone was a relative term.

"Even if you don't want to think about it right now, you're going to have to. There are already rumors going around that you and Silvermin... Well, you know. They'll probably pump your stomachs for evidence. Then it'll be like it was all for nothing!" the Rook said gleefully, stepping around to the end of the bed, claws clicking on the floor. "Then again, she might be completely gone now. I don't know. Maybe they won't find anything and it can just be your very own dirty little secret."

"I'm trying to sleep," Michael groaned, wishing he could roll over. He didn't want to think about that right then. "I'm tired."

"Yes, you would be." The Rook paused for long enough that the boy almost thought it would be quiet and let him sleep. No such luck, however. "Cannibalism is a *crime*, you know."

Oh, Michael was already aware of that fact. Very aware. He might not have known much about it before the island, but he came off it an expert.

"They're going to put you in a mock trial and sentence you. I can imagine it now. Off with their heads!"

"It wouldn't be a mock trial; they don't do those anymore. They also don't—" Michael coughed as the Rook's claws tightened around his throat. It was standing again, covered in that black cloak, its hands the only things visible besides the skull.

"Haven't I told you *not* to talk back to me? I may not be human, but I'm *very* aware of how humans operate. Understand?!" the Rook hissed. Michael tried to nod or reply, but the monster's claws around his neck hampered both of those. It seemed to get the message, however, since it slowly relaxed its grip. It drew its arms back under its cloak, standing above his bed and looking rather intimidating—but more or less harmless. Large black creatures with skulls as heads could only be scary for so long before the effect started to wear off, after all. "Now, what did I just say?"

"Off with their heads," Michael replied miserably, massaging his throat.

"Very good, Michael." He really didn't like the way it said his name, but he wasn't going to complain about anything after *that*. The Rook sat down in the chair beside his bed, looking absolutely absurd since it had to lean over slightly to allow room for its wings. Michael tried to keep his glare mild, since he didn't feel like getting more abuse. "...So what are you going to do about that?"

"What *can* I do?" he challenged quietly, averting his eyes.

"Look at me," it commanded. Michael immediately looked at it again. "*I* say you run away. It would be easy enough, since they all think you're a weak little human—which you *are*—and you could simply hide somewhere. No one would look twice at another runaway child."

"I've been on my own long enough—"

"You won't be alone!" the Rook crooned, leaning forward eagerly. "I'll help you, Michael, don't worry."

He didn't bother telling it that that was precisely what he was worried about. It would probably derive much too much satisfaction from that, anyway. "...I don't want to starve again," he said under his breath, tugging at the sheets.

"I'll make sure you don't."

"I-I don't want that!"

"Why ever not?"

"I... I want to be able to rely only on myself." It was a blatant lie, but the Rook wouldn't call him out on it. At least, he hoped not.

"...Then I'll help you. You'll have to get out of here, now, I hope you realize; you're only relying on all of these kind nurses and doctors for their help and support." Michael's mouth suddenly felt very dry. The Rook looked calmly over towards the clipboard near the door, which had all of the names of the doctors and nurses that had checked up on him when he had first been brought to the hospital. "I wouldn't want you getting *attached* to them."

Michael got the message.

An hour later, Michael was staggering down the hallway. To say he did not feel well was an understatement; he hadn't *ever* felt this bad before. His stomach was steadily trying to come up his throat, his head was pounding, and his hand hurt from where the Rook had yanked out the IV.

Speaking of the Rook, it was following behind him at a perfectly sedate pace. It didn't seem at all bothered by the time Michael was having. That didn't really surprise him, but then again, he could have hoped for a *little* bit of sympathy. The Rook seemed hell-bent on keeping Michael to itself, so why couldn't it be bothered to try to take even the tiniest amount of care of him? Not having him force-marched out of the hospital at who knew what time, blackmailing him into leaving the safety and help of the doctors and nurses by threatening to kill them...

"I hate you," Michael told the Rook, collapsing against the

nearest wall for support.

It stopped just out of kicking range (as if reading the boy's mind, however suicidal the thought probably was) and tilted its head. "What brought this on?" it asked, as if it were a perfectly casual remark.

"You—You're making me do this and you're not *helping*, for starters—" Michael had been feeling particularly malicious, mostly because his body had gotten a bit of proper nutrition for the first time in weeks, thanks to the hospital he was trying to sneak out of. He was thinking. Not clearly or rationally, as the Rook would probably gut him if it ever heard the complete version of his tirade, but thinking nonetheless, and he was thinking about how completely *unfair* it was of the Rook to demand and force him to do such horrible things and then delight in it. He probably would have even verbally attacked it for killing his parents and Tuesday. The fact that he was inching over the line into suicidal didn't even cross his mind.

The Rook had interrupted him by walking over to the nearest door, yanking it open with a bang, and walking calmly in. The sound of the beep-beep-beep from the machines the patient inside was hooked to filled the hallway. Michael looked nervously down the hall, waiting for someone to come rushing over and see what all the noise was about.

The beep-beep-beep suddenly turned into a long, drawn out beeeeeeeep. Michael nearly jumped out of his skin.

The Rook came out of the room, closed the door behind itself, muttering under its breath. The boy glared at it, hissing, "What are you *doing*?! I thought you wanted to get out of here!"

It responded by placing a clawed hand on the top of his head, continuing to whisper to itself. Michael, who had instinctively flinched back, suddenly felt a *lot* better. His stomach had settled and his headache was nothing but a memory;

it was as if he had been healed. "Feel better?" the Rook asked, probably knowing full well that he did.

"Yes... What did you—"

"Good," it interrupted. It removed its hand from his head, wrapping the black cloak around itself once more. "Now that's two."

"Huh?"

"That's two lives you've sacrificed for your own benefit," the Rook told him plainly. Michael glared at it, until its words actually sunk in. Then he felt very, very cold.

"W-Wait, did you just... *kill* someone?"

"In a way, yes."

"What do you mean, in a-a way?! You either do or you don't—!"

"If you continue raising your voice, you'll only attract attention. And you've done such a good job of sneaking out so far," it reminded him.

Michael looked down at his bare feet, hating the logic in that. Not only was the Rook right—it was now killing people again? He hadn't even known the patient in that room! But he had felt much better after the Rook had returned, so the monster had probably killed that person and somehow used that to make him healthy again.

Michael made it out of the hospital without further incident, making sure not to complain about even the slightest thing. He made a mental note to never do that again. Or, actually, it would probably be a better idea to never get close to anyone ever again, at least not if he didn't want to see them killed. He glanced over his shoulder at where the Rook was still following him mutely. It had already killed his parents—he wouldn't put it past the monster to have killed the entire ship—and Tuesday and the nameless patient that had just died for his sake.

And, for some reason, it had spared Silvermin.

He didn't want to think about that, however, since the Rook had the annoying habit of somehow knowing what he was thinking occasionally. If Silvermin had gotten out of the cycle of death by chance, he wasn't going to mention it and have the Rook end up killing him, too. Maybe it had only spared him because it had been Tuesday he'd spent the most time with, not the businessman.

Either way, Michael was sure not to tell the Rook any of that. If Silvermin could get out of the situation without a monster or without dying, good for him. At least one of them could.

"You're going to want to get some clothes. The hospital gown isn't terribly inconspicuous," the Rook pointed out, jarring him out of his thoughts. Michael glanced back over his shoulder again at it. "I'd suggest getting as far as you can from the hospital, too. They'll probably start a search for you once they know you're missing. We wouldn't want anyone finding you, now would we, Michael?"

He sighed. "No, we wouldn't."

One high-tension night turned into the next high tension day. With a bit of help from the Rook, however, Michael managed not to get captured. Days turned into weeks, and weeks steadily turned into months. The search for the boy started to die down.

And so, months gradually turned to years.

Four years later, Michael looked completely different. No longer was he the angel that Tuesday assumed he was. The Rook had changed him too much.

When he was ten, Michael had been short, had plenty of baby fat left, and had blue eyes and bright blond hair. Now he had grown, retained the starved look the island had given him, and had black hair. The Rook had done that to him, after he had commented offhandedly that it was hard to evade searchers with his blond hair; it had ran its fingers through his hair a few times, and the next morning, Michael had woken up with black hair.

The only thing he retained was his blue eyes, but even those had subtle differences—he had the beginnings of crow's feet at fourteen, had bags under them more often than not, and it was clear he had been on his own for far too long.

Living in nothing short of the wilderness with only the Rook there had taken its toll. It was true that it would offer to help him occasionally, usually by pointing out a suitable shelter to sleep in or killing animals to eat. Michael knew that the Rook could kill anything it wanted to, though he also had realized that it didn't need to *do* anything to kill. Just like that night in the hospital, the Rook would wander off while muttering to itself, and come back with birds, rabbits, squirrels, and once, even a deer.

Michael was not a picky eater. He never had been much of one, but having to fend for himself had certainly erased any of that. Whenever the Rook was kind enough to bring him food, he ate it.

During this time, the pair had been working steadily north. Michael had initially wanted to escape any would-be 'rescuers', but he had also wanted to escape the tropical climate. Humidity, palm trees, and sand all reminded him far too much of the island.

"I want to go back to the city," Michael said one day, out of the blue. The Rook looked up from where it was contentedly skinning a rabbit. It didn't ask him why.

Instead, it said, "You'll meet people there."

"I won't care about them. If I meet them, I won't give my name or anything about myself; they'll just see me as a stranger."

Michael, who had been staring into the fire, looked up at the Rook. "I won't get attached. You won't have to kill anyone."

"Good," it hummed, tossing the animal's pelt into the fire.

Michael absently bit his nails. It was a habit he had gotten into since meeting the Rook—one of many, actually. He glanced down at the burning fur, wrinkling his nose at the smell. He'd tried to tan pelts before to make clothing, and had never liked the smell; it was much easier to just have the Rook bring him new clothes whenever his current ones got torn up. "…You have no objections?" he asked, mildly surprised by that. Usually, the Rook shot down any ideas that involved other humans.

"Do you want me to say no?" the Rook asked, tilting its skull up in his direction. It tossed the rabbit's head at him.

"No, but… Rook, what do *you* eat?" It was a question that had been asked many, many times, but each time, the answer seemed to change. Michael had never seen the creature eat, however. Maybe it was the lack of a working jaw (or bottom jaw), or maybe the Rook ate something that wasn't so tangible as small animals.

"Your company is enough to sate my hunger, Michael," it responded cheerfully, throwing the rest of the slightly mangled corpse at the boy.

He sighed. "Right."

The next morning, Michael finished off the remains of the rabbit—the Rook watched him silently during the entire meal, which was unnerving, but thankfully nothing new—and put out the fire. He'd accidentally set quite a few things on fire, and was very careful with it as a result. He might not have more than a third grade education, but he knew the things that allowed him to stay alive.

"Where are you going to be going?" the Rook asked. They had passed through towns and villages before, of course, but they had always skirted around the bigger cities. Michael savored those times, because if he came in contact with another person, the Rook would hide. Come to think of it, the Rook was now fairly passive on the matter, but it *had* to know that it couldn't be seen...

"I don't know. I just want to go to the city and see civilization again." Not to mention he wanted some actual food. Even if he didn't have any money, he could always beg or steal or pickpocket... The Rook must be rubbing off on him. Michael shook his head, trying to keep his morals above water. He'd resort to begging for food or money, but not stealing.

Maybe.

"Are you going to be following me?" Michael asked, hoping for a negative answer.

"Why, of course, Michael. It hurts me to know that you'd think I'd leave after all we've been through," the Rook replied with a mock sigh.

"You're going to get seen. You can't just walk through an entire city of people looking like a monster."

"Now I'm even more hurt, Michael. Do you intend to hurt me?" The Rook closed the distance between them with too few steps, leaning over Michael to make the height difference that much worse. The dark-haired boy wanted to look away, but knew it would only earn him pain. He slowly shook his head. "If you must know, I don't plan on staying like this for long. Do you really believe I've gotten through this much of my life without being able to walk among humans?"

Michael, who was accustomed to the Rook shifting randomly between its two-legged form and four-legged, animal-like form, was somewhat unsurprised to hear that it had a way of concealing itself. "...Can you go invisible?" If so, he really didn't want to be near the Rook any longer. It meant that he really couldn't *ever* get away from it.

"What? No. Of course not; that's silly." He couldn't help the relieved sigh that followed. The Rook shifted, looking slightly miffed. It reached up with its claws to grab its skull—and it was then that Michael realized it didn't have its scaly, bird-like hands any longer. It was true that its nails were still slightly sharpened, but they were *human* hands.

"Oh God," Michael hissed, taking a step back instinctively.

The Rook took off its skull as if it were a mask. And, it seemed, it really *was* one—at least, it was now. What lay behind the bone and horn was a perfectly human face, albeit one that still reminded Michael so utterly of the Rook it was amazing he had dealt with it for four years without seeing it. No, *him*, since it was a very male face that stared with dark eyes down at him, black hair swept back, save for one lock that hung down over his nose.

"See, Michael? I am perfectly capable of blending in with you humans," the Rook said, grinning.

Defensively and trying to get over the shock, Michael immediately pointed out in a flat tone, "You still have wings. Humans don't have wings!"

He looked over his shoulder, surprised to see the large, black wings still there. "Oh yeah."

After sorting out various problems in the Rook's disguise—the wings weren't the only problem, since Michael soon noticed feathers in his hair and he didn't think he had to get rid of his tail, either—Michael breathed a sigh of relief. It was odd to the extreme, having to take care of the Rook and seeing his *expressions* for the first time, especially as the new human-thing didn't have much control over them. He had spent so long staring at an impassive skull that he was entirely unused to grins, snarls, raised eyebrows, and even a roll of the eyes."

"If you didn't feel the need to nitpick—"

"If *you* could create a proper human body!" Michael cut across, though it earned him a none-too-kind cuff to the back of the head.

"My body is *fine*. Look at this!" The Rook flexed his arms before gesturing vaguely to the rest of his body.

"Why do I care—" He outright growled and the Rook hit him again.

"You better care, Michael. I'm all you have in the world, remember?" he said coldly, pulling his stolen shirt back over his head. Michael looked away, though he technically was forbidden to. He didn't need reminding, though.

Predictably, he was hit again. He didn't bother replying, instead fixing the back of the Rook's head with a watery-eyed glare.

"Well? Come on. You want to go to this city of yours, so let's hurry up. I'd like to get this over with as quickly as possible."

"...You *know* I want to stay there. I want to go back to humanity," Michael said softly, following along in the Rook's shadow. The Rook didn't look back at him and instead stretched his arms up over his head.

"You'll get tired of them soon enough." It sounded less like a casual remark and more like a warning, at least to Michael's trained ears. "I'm all the company you need."

The boy grunted in response.

The Rook paused in mid-step, turning back to look over his shoulder. "Aren't I, Michael?" he asked, voice deceptively light.

"Of course you are." With that blatant lie, the Rook turned back and continued walking. Michael squinted at his back. He still moved with vaguely jerky movements, mirroring his actions in his other forms. In human form, however, it made him look less like a monster and more like a child trying to learn how to walk properly.

Still, all it took was a lie to keep the Rook happy. Michael didn't know if he knew it was a lie or if he actually took it as a truth, but he wasn't going to ask either way.

No one looked twice at the two scraggly-looking travelers walking into the city. They might have stared a bit that initial look, but there were no double takes, at least.

Michael still felt nervous. He felt himself break out into a cold sweat. He felt the eyes on him from every angle, silently judging him and evaluating him and wondering if he was the blond boy who had run away from a southern hospital all those years ago. He set his mouth in a firm line and tried not to think of it, but every girl with dark hair he passed, every man in a business suit checking his watch, every mother and father walking with a child between them... He was used to the sensation of this pressure in smaller towns and villages they had stopped at before, but the fact that he wasn't leaving in a couple hours (hopefully) seemed to make it worse.

The Rook put an arm around his shoulders.

Michael didn't jump, but he did turn to look up at the man walking casually beside him. The Rook didn't look at him and instead was staring ahead. Michael did notice the faint smirk, however.

The boy huffed, but didn't make any motion to move. He didn't like it, but he really would like to avoid causing some sort of scene—or more physical abuse in general, which he would undoubtedly receive if he didn't let the Rook have his way (yet again).

"What are you planning on doing in this city of yours,

Michael?" the Rook asked after a bit of time had elapsed. He was still not looking at the boy, instead tilting his head back to look at the tall buildings. "Humans have come a long ways…"

"I want to get some food."

"You ate this morning."

"Humans eat several times a day, remember?" It was a bit sad that Michael had to remind the Rook this.

"Where do you want to eat, then? There seems to be plenty of places in this city of yours." He could sense that the phrase 'city of yours' would become a recurring theme.

"We need money first. Food isn't free. Have any ideas?" Michael asked sarcastically. The Rook shrugged.

"We could ask." With that, the Rook withdrew his arm and marched off, verbally assaulting a harried-looking man with a briefcase. Michael could only stand and watched, amazed. Not only did the Rook come back after a couple minutes with a fistful of cash, but the Rook had done something *selfless*. And helpful. It was true that he had helped Michael on a couple occasions before, but usually it involved the killing of some defenseless creature.

Michael watched in nothing short of awe as the businessman walked away, not bleeding, not broken, not dead. The Rook grinned and held out the money, clearly having no idea what to do next with it. "H-How did you—?!"

"I told him I'd kill him if he didn't give me all of his money. Is this enough for your food?" he asked eagerly, dumping it in Michael's hands. The boy looked down at the money, not bothering to count it but seeing a fifty-dollar bill in amongst the others.

"…I'm pretty sure that's illegal."

"For humans."

He didn't bother arguing. After all, what could he do?

Teach human laws and morals to a monster? He would only end up bleeding because of it. Plus, the Rook *hadn't* hurt the man, at least, and they *had* gotten money out of the deal. Even if it was illegal.

As if sensing this, the Rook leaned down, set one arm on each of Michael's shoulders, and touched their foreheads together. Grinning hard, he whispered, "Eating Tuesday was illegal, too."

"Get off of me," Michael snapped, pushing him away while ignoring the chill that went down his spine. The Rook dragged his claws along the sides of Michael's neck as he removed his arms.

"You're snappy. We should go eat," he told him innocently, flicking the droplets of blood off his fingers. Michael, holding his neck, glared sullenly up at him. "You always get like this when you're hungry. It's okay, though, I forgive you." The Rook often said that, but somehow, it was much more disturbing when accompanied by a bright smile and a tilt of the head.

Michael, being the slightly more sane and definitely more social or the two, had to go in to a fast food restaurant and order. He didn't bother getting anything for the Rook, since he didn't appear to eat anything anyway. He still felt awkward standing in line by himself, though. Even if he'd aged four years, sometimes, he still felt like the young boy on the island.

The pair sat outside at one of the tables. The Rook hummed to himself and swung his legs underneath his chair, chin in his hands. Michael ate in silence, savoring the taste of greasy, fatty, hot French fries. He could barely remember the flavor, but oh, it was *good*. He barely noticed when the Rook reached over to steal one of his. He did notice, however, when he said, "These are actually pretty good."

"...I thought you didn't eat," Michael said warily. He

wasn't sure what the Rook was playing at now.

"I never said that," the Rook denied around a mouthful of fries. And, actually, he *had*, and on numerous occasions, too.

"Will you be able to eat human food?" Michael had always gotten the impression that the Rook ate non-human food. What that may actually be, he had no clue whatsoever. But he would not doubt it if he fed on things like souls or something.

Michael shivered at the very thought and hastily murmured a prayer under his breath. He could barely remember anything but Our Father, and did it more out of habit than anything else since the Rook (while obviously a demon of some sort) paid him no heed whenever he attempted it, but it reassured him a bit nonetheless.

"I have a human body, so why shouldn't I be able to eat human food?" the Rook asked conversationally, stealing more fries. Michael wanted to keep them to himself, but he knew what hunger was like and what it made people do. The Rook was bad enough without the added effect of wanting food.

"You don't have a human body. You had wings just a couple of hours ago."

"That's irrelevant. I can ask any person on this street my species, and they would all agree that I'm completely human. Are you just angry, Michael? Don't want to share with me anymore?" The Rook looked significantly less intimidating with a French fry sticking out of his mouth.

"You're not *breathing*. That might give it away," Michael deadpanned.

"...Oh yeah." The Rook sucked in a deep breath, held it for a moment, then exhaled. Grinning, he said, "There."

"No, humans do it all the time. Not just once—constantly." Michael was hoping to play off his lack of patience and possibly get rid of him for a little while. He didn't have very high expectations for that, however, since the Rook always managed to get things his way.

The Rook practiced breathing, which was odd to watch and made the dark-haired boy quite attuned to his own. They got a few weird looks, too, random passerby wondering why a grown man was apparently hyperventilating. It wasn't until the food was all gone that the human wannabe got the hang of it, and even then, Michael could tell (with no small amount of satisfaction) that he had to concentrate on it.

"How do you talk if you don't breathe?"

"Talking is just moving vocal chords. Sounds I know."

Michael shrugged to himself and continued walking, hands in his pockets. Beside him, the Rook practiced his breathing, earning them even more looks. The younger of the two took the opportunity to marvel at the city sights. It had been a long time since he had seen so many people in such a small amount of space, and the tall buildings all around them made the enclosed feeling even more acute.

He had grown up in a small town, so it wasn't a feeling of returning home he was getting. It was more a feeling of returning to humanity—and what could be more human than a polluted, overpopulated city?

The Rook stopped suddenly. Michael didn't notice, eyes instead on the skyscrapers. He noticed, however, when the Rook's hand clamped down on his shoulder, halting him, nails digging a bit into his shirt. "I didn't do anything wrong," Michael said immediately, heart pounding from the abruptness of the stop.

"...There's someone here," the Rook said quietly, completely immobile save his eyes.

"It's a city, there's going to be a lot of people here."

"Shut *up* Michael. There's something not *human* here," he

snapped, still looking. All around them, however, people bustled past, not minding the two stopped on the sidewalk. No monsters, no skull-masked looming things—which meant that it had to be another human-looking one. Michael swallowed thickly.

"There are *more* of you?" he whispered.

"Unfortunately," he replied shortly. The Rook continued in his search.

Just then, when the Rook's eyes had darted skyward, Michael saw someone burst out of the crowd around them. Immediately, the Rook grabbed him and jumped into the air, wings already out and beating for more altitude. People scattered below them, shouting and screaming—all except for two. All Michael could make out was light hair on both of them and the annoyance positively radiating from them both.

Then the Rook passed a building and they were out of sight.

CHAPTER FIVE

If I Should **Die** Before I **Wake**

"Why didn't you tell me there are more of you?" Michael demanded shakily, after they were safe once more. The Rook had been unusually silent since the incident, only speaking once he was sure that they really *were* safe. Or, rather, that Michael was safe.

The Rook looked up, narrowing his eyes a bit. "There aren't more of *me*; there is only one Rook." Michael should have heard the warning in his voice, but he was too shook up over being flown over the city and out into the forest on the northern side of it. The Rook had never been so physical with him. Abusive, yes, but being *carried* for two hours straight was a little nerve-wracking. Especially taking into account the fact that he had been carried hundreds of feet in the air and by a monster that regularly took pleasure in his pain.

"Then what are you, Rook? What *are* you things?! Why were they chasing you—who were they?"

"Humans like to call us demons, or witches if we're looking like you, or angels or anything they feel like. We don't *have* a human name." Michael couldn't help but snort at the 'angels' bit. The Rook was the furthest thing from an angel possible. "And for your information, Michael, I am being chased because I committed a crime."

"That's not news—"

"Fine, Michael, would you like me to repeat this particular crime? You may think that I've been cruel up until now, but *oh no*, not at all!" Suddenly, the boy's head was slammed against the nearest tree, cheek scraping against the rough bark. Michael hadn't seen the attack coming. "Tell me, Michael, have I ripped off your head? Have I dug my nails into your eye sockets and had to pull and yank and wrench it sideways until it comes clean off your neck? Have I listened to your spinal cord snap? Have I left your body behind to rot and have I *stolen your skull*, Michael?!"

Michael gasped out a "n-no!" as he struggled to stay conscious. He had to close his eye to prevent the blood from his head getting into it. He could barely process what the Rook was saying to him, even after the demon let go of him and let him drop to the ground.

"I think I've been perfectly kind to you, Michael. Don't you talk back to me and tell me how ungrateful you think you are. You are only alive today because of me."

Michael didn't answer, since he had passed out.

When Michael awoke, he awoke to a headache and almost-concerned black eyes staring down at him. He squeezed his eyes shut again with a groan, head pounding terribly. His hands went up to it, dimly remembering blood, and was surprised to find his fingers touch fabric. A bandage.

He opened his eyes again, this time looking directly at the Rook. He had never bandaged any of the wounds he had inflicted before. It was true that Michael rarely lost consciousness from them, but this hadn't been the first time.

The Rook didn't apologize, and instead forced the boy into a sitting position. Michael grunted and held his head, dizzy. "...How long was I out this time?" he asked, unable to resist adding the last part or to hide the bitterness in his voice.

"It's almost sunrise. We'll have to move soon. Those two trackers will catch up to us before long," the Rook said tonelessly. He stood up and stretched his arms and wings.

"Why didn't you just... move yourself?"

"You were bleeding and I didn't want you making a trail

for them to follow." Michael frowned, sensing a lie. Why, though, he couldn't say. "Come on. They'll be here soon."

"How do you know that? You flew for hours," he mumbled, putting his head in his hands to try to stop it from hurting so much.

"They may not be able to fly, but they're fast. And I can feel them in the area." The Rook's voice was still flat and hollow and reminded Michael of Silvermin's voice when they had reached that decision on the island.

"Why are you waiting, then? Let's go." He didn't feel nearly as alright with that as he sounded, though. In fact, he wouldn't mind sleeping another ten hours.

But, of course, staying there meant he met more creatures like the Rook, which was something he did *not* want to do under any circumstances. One was bad enough. He didn't need two more in his life.

The Rook picked Michael up again and they took to the skies once more. The altitude, wind rushing past his ears, and the chill of the morning did nothing to help his headache, but he just buried his face in the Rook's shirt and tried his hardest to ignore that. They flew all day, until Michael mentioned he was hungry, and after the Rook killed him an owl, he hurried him through the meal and they flew through the night, too. Michael found it difficult to fly in those conditions, and could only doze occasionally throughout the flight.

It was sunset of the second day that they stopped for good. Michael was stiff, sore, hungry, tired, and cranky, but thankful when his feet touched solid ground once more. He glanced up at the setting sun directly in front of them. He didn't bother asking why the Rook had decided to take him west, however.

Things were awkward between them after that. Michael didn't know what to say, and the Rook likewise kept silent. He never would have guessed that the Rook was being hunted by others—or even that there *were* others. Or that he had done such a thing to one of his brethren.

They didn't come across the two hunters again, however. It seemed as though the Rook's change of direction threw them off the scent, at least for a while. The days passed slowly this time, and Michael found himself wanting to go back to humanity more and more again. He didn't mention it, however; he didn't know how the Rook would react.

It was after the first week had passed that Michael realized what the Rook was doing to himself.

"Are you sleeping?" Michael asked on the day that the Rook collapsed. The man, lying on his back with his wings splayed out awkwardly, glared up at him.

"Of course not."

"You have to," Michael replied primly. "You have a human body now, don't you? Those require sleep."

"I'm *not* human."

"You're breathing this time. Your body is going to get run down by that, even. Humans get tired out very easily, remember?" The Rook, when not human, often loved to point this out to Michael.

"I'm not human, Michael, *remember*?" he echoed, lightly closing his eyes. "And I'm only breathing half the time. I keep forgetting to."

"Then what have you been doing at night?"

"...Flying, on the lookout for those two..." Michael didn't fail to notice that his voice was getting softer as he continued speaking. He didn't reopen his eyes, either.

"That will tire you out. You should go to sleep. Just take a nap, just a quick little rest," he whispered as he leaned in. If the Rook fell asleep, then he could feasibly get away. If only for a few hours, Michael could be *alone*. He might get the beating of his life for it, but the thought of it was much too tempting.

"...No, I'm fine," the Rook argued, eyes still closed. He had stopped breathing, which meant he probably *was* tired. Michael could sympathize; after the island, he'd had nightmares so bad they had kept him up for several days straight. Never a week, though, and he had never fallen over in the middle of the afternoon because of them.

"Liar." The fact that he immediately didn't have talons buried into any part of him attested to how tired the Rook really was. "Go to sleep or you'll end up dying."

"No... won't..." He was fading fast, but still stubborn. Michael almost smiled at the vain attempt. Almost.

"What if you're flying? You can't fly with no sleep. Just take a nap. A little nap," he whispered soothingly, physically resisting the urge to brush the lone lock of black hair back. Michael chalked it up to the only motherly presence in his life he remembered: Tuesday. She had often done the same to Michael as he fell asleep. "You'll fall if you're flying," he added, dropping his voice even further.

"You'll..."

Michael never found out what he would supposedly do, because the Rook was completely asleep at that point. The boy experimentally stood up and took a couple steps back, expecting him to jump back to his feet and tackle him for trying to leave. No such thing happened, however. He took another few steps backward, tense, ready to bolt or defend. The Rook remained motionless (and still not breathing), wings still splayed, one hand idly on his chest.

Michael tripped.

He yelped as he went down and banged the back of his head against the tree whose root had tripped him. Biting his lip and trying to ignore the pain, Michael was astounded as he looked up and found the Rook still on the ground, asleep.

After the inadvertent test and discovering that apparently, demons were sound sleepers, and for the first time in four years, Michael left the Rook.

Unfortunately, the worst thing possible happened during that time. Michael had ran off from the sleeping Rook, heart nearly bursting with excitement as the thought *I'm free I'm alone I'm free* raced through his head. He tripped several more times and scraped his hands and face on numerous branches that he'd probably have to explain later. When his lungs were burning and his throat was raw as they desperately tried to get the rest of his body enough oxygen during his sprint, Michael found himself break out into the forest and into a meadow. The sun shone cheerfully overhead, smiling down at him and the flowers and the bugs and the birds and everything that was not the Rook.

Michael screamed, throwing his arms out and falling into the waist-high grass. His yell eventually died off and turned into a hoarse laugh. He hadn't laughed in far too long—at least not a real laugh. He had been compliant to the Rook's whims and wishes for far too long. Now he could do what he *wanted*, at least for a little while, and not have to care a single bit about the Rook until he woke up.

He curled up in the grasses and let himself breathe, valuing it and marveling at how the Rook could do without it. The air was unbearably fresh and sweet. A bumblebee buzzed lazily overhead, not sparing Michael a moment of its busy time. He reached up for it, though, missing by miles.

He let his eyelids droop, though he was far too awake to even entertain the thought of sleeping. He wasn't going to waste one nap with another. It was just so calming, not having to watch his back constantly, not having to cater to a monster, not having to nurse bruises and cuts and worry about receiving new ones. It was nice not having the Rook's abuse hanging over his head.

Of course, Michael had underestimated the Rook.

He also had overestimated himself. He had been just ten when his parents had died, and just ten when he had lost Tuesday and left Silvermin as well. He had never returned home to any of his friends or extended family. For every single day since the ship went down, Michael had the Rook instead.

And every single day for four years in a young boy's life left a profound impact on said boy.

He had already lost most of his memories of his childhood and was left only remnants. He could vividly remember his mother's terrified face as they faced the burning boat, but he could not remember her smile anymore. He remembered his father marching down the beach and Silvermin restraining him, but he could not remember what the last words he'd spoken were. He couldn't recall his best friend's face. He likewise couldn't bring up much of his home, or what had been his home prior to that fated trip.

Michael, when he thought of the term 'motherly', instead saw Tuesday smoothing back his hair and calling him an angel. He couldn't get Silvermin's voice out of his head when he had told them what would have to happen.

Then, past that, it was all the Rook.

Michael opened his eyes and sat up, glaring at the nearest flower. He was free of that monster, at least for a little while, and he was all he could think about? That was hardly fair. It was true that many things in his life hadn't been fair up until that point, but at least they had been survivable. If Michael was actually *missing* the Rook, he...

Well, he wasn't sure what he'd do, but it would be drastic and probably something he'd regret when he came to his senses and decided that he didn't really miss the Rook's company and he was only adjusting to his freedom anyway and was only thinking about him because subconsciously he was worried about what would happen when the demon woke up and—

Michael groaned and pushed his palms into his eyes, head tilting back. When he started mentally rambling, he knew something major was wrong.

So he decided to ignore the problem as best he could. He stood up, dusted off his pants, and waded through the meadow. The farther away from the Rook he could get, the better. He'd have hell to pay later for it, but that was later. He couldn't help the notion that if he was getting hit or scratched and the Rook was snarling at him, things would be normal again. The Rook wouldn't sleep for that long, or that often, so this hopefully wouldn't happen again.

Michael made it to the other side of the meadow without much change in attitude. He was, however, covered in pollen and extremely thankful he wasn't allergic to it. He sat down in the grass, this time crossing his legs and using his arms as support as he leaned back. Not much time had passed, though it already felt like an eternity. It was just so *quiet* and *safe* without the Rook constantly around.

…Or, at least, it was quiet.

Michael was somewhat disturbed to find himself feeling nervous. The Rook had always watched out for him before, at least in his own way, and made sure that the only threat to Michael had been from himself. Now the boy didn't have that assurance, for the first time in years. He felt skittish. He was a fourteen-year-old alone in a forest with no way of calling for help and very little knowledge of how to defend himself (he never bothered against the Rook). The only thing he had going for himself was a possessive supernatural bodyguard who was, for all intents and purposes, dead to the world at that moment.

"This is stupid," he muttered to himself, tilting his chin back to try to get more sunlight on his neck. It was a bizarre feeling that was going to drive him insane soon, feeling relaxed and overly tense at the same time. Moreover, he couldn't stop thinking about the Rook, who was snoozing who knew how far away and without a care in the world. For once, Michael didn't matter to him.

And that really, really bothered him.

As much as he hated to admit it, he found he enjoyed the Rook's company (when he wasn't killing people or hurting Michael) and the protection he offered gave him some peace of mind. He could sleep at night safely with that knowledge and ever-present company.

The sun was blotted out and Michael could immediately feel the temperature difference. He cracked open an eye to glare at the offending cloud. It had been so clear earlier; if it started literally raining on his parade, he would be angry, to say the least. It also meant the Rook would probably wake up at that point, realize he was missing, and that would be the end of his forced vacation.

It was frustrating. On one hand, he very much would like to be away from the Rook and enjoy his time alone. On the other hand, he really *didn't* like to be away from the Rook and he was getting antsy about being by himself. Then again, he would be antsy when he had to return and explain that he'd left—Michael decided he really shouldn't have done this in the first place. It was only going to get him into trouble.

Just enough of his inner turmoil disappeared when the sun came out again, warming him once more. It was the little things like that made this trip worthwhile. Michael smiled slightly to himself, tilting his head back once more. His arms were starting to get sore, but the rest of him liked it too much to move.

He had no idea how long he sat there, basking in the sunlight and listening to the rustle of the grasses around him accompanied by the sporadic bursts of music from songbirds. Occasionally the sun would get covered by a cloud, though, which irritated him, both for the lack of immediate warmth and worry for the weather later that night.

Finally, the sun was blotted out, and it remained that way. Michael groaned and flopped onto his back. He knew it was getting to be later in the afternoon, but he wasn't ready to let go of his break yet. He didn't want to return to the Rook (he just wished he had never left). With a half-hearted yawn, he sat up again, rubbing at his eyes as he opened them.

The sun had not been blotted out by a cloud. Michael stared up at the two figures standing over him, casting their shadows on him.

"You're Rook's new pet, hmm?" the man asked, crouching down until he was eye-level with Michael. He smiled brightly. He glanced up at his partner, amber eyes practically glowing in the afternoon light. "Look what we've found, Wolf. What do you think we should do?"

The woman still standing over them said nothing, only crossing her arms. Her hair was steel grey and her eyes were a cold blue, but there was nothing old about her. The Wolf looked just as young as the man beside Michael did.

"Where's the Rook?" the man asked without needing an answer. His eyes were fixed on Michael now, looking very much like the cat that had just caught the mouse.

"I-I don't know," Michael lied. He wasn't particularly fond of the Rook, but he wasn't going to give up his protection out of spite.

The man grabbed a fistful of the boy's black hair and stood

up, dragging him up with him. "Do you hear that? He doesn't know. Hmm, hmm. That's not right—the Rook wouldn't *dare* leave you alone, now would he? Come on out, you stupid bird! Come play!" he shouted. Michael winced, knowing that the Rook wouldn't come. He was too far away and probably still asleep. He was on his own with the two.

"He's not here," the Wolf spoke up, voice low and husky. She looked casually across the meadow. "He can't hide in this situation. He would hide in the trees, not grass."

"Hmm, you're right," he replied absently, voice sounding disturbingly like a purr. "But if there's one thing I know about that damned bird, it's that he's good with sounds."

"H-He's not here. He left m-me. He knows you're following him, and..." And what? Michael didn't know. He knew, though, that the Rook wasn't coming, that he was on his own, and that he had to figure a way out of this. The Rook may not want to kill him, but these two didn't seem to have any qualms about that. "Please, let me go." Begging hadn't ever done him any good in the past, but it didn't hurt to try.

Surprisingly, the fair-haired man let him go. Michael stumbled back, shaking his head to try to get rid of the stinging. The Wolf and her accomplice stared evenly at him. They seemed to be waiting for something.

"...Go on, get."

That was it—they were expecting him to run back to the Rook. Michael backed up another few steps, having no problem with putting some distance between them, but did they *really* think he was stupid enough to literally lead them to him? Not likely. Chances were that they would catch the Rook and then dispose of Michael just to not leave any loose human ties. He wasn't going to give up his demonic protection, and he wasn't going to give up his life, either.

There must have been some change in his demeanor to signal that decision, or maybe the monsters were just abnormally good at reading minds. The Wolf sprang forward with a snarl, catching Michael around the middle with one arm and pinning him to the ground in the next instant. "He's not going to be easy, Cat," she growled, glancing back over her shoulder at the man.

He strolled languidly over, hands in his pockets. "I can see that. *That's* a shame. We'll have to go back to Plan A."

Slightly winded and fully terrified, Michael struggled. The woman's grasp was like iron, however, and he couldn't budge an inch. They'd kill him to get to the Rook, and the monster in question was currently sleeping. And all he had wanted out of the day was a couple hours to himself, too. "Please—don't—"

The Cat sat down beside him with a smug smile. He gently picked up Michael's hand, petting it. Then, without warning, he snapped the wrist.

He screamed. The Cat grinned; the Wolf winced at the sound. Michael's scream faded into the forest, upsetting many of the birds he'd been listening to earlier. Unfortunately, none of them was the Rook.

The two waited patiently for their quarry to appear, but of course, he didn't. Michael couldn't help but hope that the sound had woken him, but he'd been shouting and yelling earlier, even when he'd been right next to him. He wasn't holding out too much hope for a sudden rescue.

"That's a shame," the Cat repeated, sounding slightly disappointed. He moved his hands up further along Michael's arm. The boy sucked in a breath, knowing what was coming next. This time, the crack wasn't nearly as audible, but the pain was much worse. Michael didn't scream, though. He didn't know whether it was pride or forsaken hope that made him grit his teeth and muffle any sound.

"He's already learned how to deal with you, Cat," the Wolf spat, eyes suddenly bright. She grinned, revealing sharp teeth. "I'm taking over."

"That's no fun," the Cat complained. He didn't make any move to stop her, however.

The Wolf leapt to her feet and pulled Michael up by the front of his shirt. She grabbed his injured arm and wrenched it savagely behind his back. He growled in pain but managed not to open his mouth. She frowned. Michael looked away and kept his mouth clamped shut. Maybe it was pride at this point that was making him do that. He still wasn't sure.

He jumped, however, when she threw her head back and *howled*. It wasn't human sounding in the least, nor was it completely canine. His ears rang from it, and by the look of it, the Cat didn't enjoy it much, either. Both males kept silent, however, until the Wolf finished. She then turned coolly to Michael, not smiling any longer. "Call him."

"No." He didn't even go to the trouble of pretending like he couldn't.

"Call him or I will rip your throat out with my teeth." Her voice dropped in pitch until it was nothing short of a bark towards the end. She leaned in towards Michael, pressing her forehead against his. This time, she whispered, "I will get the Rook here in one of two ways. You will either call him now, or I will rip out your throat and paint the meadow with your blood until he notices the stench."

Michael swallowed thickly. His arm gave him a painful throb to remind him that they were serious. This was serious—he could very easily lose his life in the next few moments depending on what he did. Was he *really* going to die just to protect the Rook?

"R-Rook," he croaked, voice raw. It was barely audible.

Immediately, a black form hit the Wolf with enough force to send them tumbling. Michael, suddenly released, stood shakily and watched with horror as the two fought. The Rook was back in his full demon form, smashing his skull's horns into the Wolf's side. Michael could hear the cracks even from where he was. The Wolf kicked him off her and leapt at him, turning into a beast mid-flight. Unlike the Rook's black body covered with fine, fur-like feathers, a body that only vaguely resembled his namesake, the Wolf was immediately recognizable as one.

She also had her own skull, Michael couldn't help but notice.

Beside him, a tan feline with a matching skull launched himself at the Rook, only to be smacked by the Wolf as she was thrown into him. The two got back to their feet and stayed away from the Rook this time, circling around him warily. The Rook watched them both stonily, wings tensed at his sides.

The Wolf snapped her jaws together angrily, jerking her head towards the Cat. He nodded, and they both sprang at the Rook. He responded by taking to the air, his feet narrowly missing the claws that tried to follow him.

"If you run away from us now, we will snap the boy's neck," the Cat called, tail curling in Michael's direction. He felt cold and backed up, only to wince as his arm reminded him of its very injured presence. The Rook didn't reply or make any motion to indicate he'd heard the threat. It wasn't exactly reassuring.

He didn't run away, at least.

"What are you going to do, Rook? You're outmatched—you've always been a coward, anyway! Will you really stay and fight to protect your pet?" the Cat purred, taking a step towards Michael. The Rook responded with a screech and dive-bombed him. The Cat snarled and tried to turn in time to defend himself, but couldn't; the airborne attacker slammed into his side and threw him several yards across the meadow, well away from Michael.

The Wolf had caught up to the Rook before he could take flight again, however. She caught one of his hind legs in her jaws and tried to forcibly rip him out of the skies. For his part, he tried to lift them both or kick her off. Eventually, he stopped trying and instead landing on top of her, effectively dislodging her from his leg.

By that time, however, the Cat had recovered and took a running leap at them, hitting the Rook's wings and pinning them to his back with teeth and claws. Fur and feathers were literally flying as the Rook tried to dislodge him. His wings were stronger than the Cat's awkward grip on him and he managed to knock him off. The Rook kicked the Wolf in the jaw for good measure before she could sneak up on him from behind, and then whirled around, backed up, and faced them squarely.

"I will kill you both," he said simply, speaking for the first time.

The Cat laughed. The Wolf didn't reply.

CHAPTER SIX

Do As **Done** And There Is **Nothing Left To Be**

Michael had no idea how the Rook could win against two of his own kind. It was true that he seemed to untouchable, invincible to him—but he was just a human. He didn't have claws or sharp teeth or a skull for a head. He couldn't come close to the power the demons all possessed.

The Cat and Wolf circled the Rook, tails lashing. None of them were that well off anymore. The Wolf had a bloody mess for a side; the Cat was having trouble walking steadily; the Rook completely off one leg. Michael knew that the odds of two on one were not fair and not good. Even if the Rook had the sky and wings to fight with, he had to get into the air to take advantage of that.

"I'll snap those hollow bones of yours, bird!" the Cat called, a grin in his voice. The Rook muttered something under his non-existent breath in response.

When the Rook continued mumbling, however, something struck Michael as odd. Or rather, discordant. Something wasn't right about the image of the Rook muttering a continuous stream of unknown things. The Rook wasn't subtle or quiet; he was harsh and loud.

Michael noticed that the Cat and Wolf had stopped circling. Their tattered ears, poking out from underneath the skulls, rotated forward to hear. Their tails had even stopped moving; both of them were completely motionless, listening to the Rook. Michael's breath hitched; he knew where he had heard that mutter before. Right before the Rook killed the patient at the hospital.

"Are you *insane*?!" the Cat suddenly yowled, catching onto this fact at about the same time. His visibly bristled and even hissed. The Wolf, too, had her hackles raised and was backing up, tail tucked between her legs. "You—You'll kill your pet, too!"

The Rook didn't respond and only kept talking to himself, though his voice was beginning to rise in volume.

The Wolf recoiled until she was behind the Cat. "…We may have to leave. We did not expect him to do this, Cat," she growled.

"No! He's bluffing. He won't kill his human—he wouldn't dare!" he snapped at her, jaws clicking. She bowed her head but didn't reply, so the Cat took the initiative and ran at the Rook. The Rook responded by leaping into the air and hovering above them, chanting in an audible voice now. The language wasn't one Michael recognized or understood. The Cat circled below him a couple times, bushy tail lashing angrily once more.

"Come. Let's leave," the Wolf tried again. "This isn't worth getting killed."

"You better listen to her, Cat," the Rook interrupted himself, pointing down at the feline with one claw. "You're forgetting something important!"

The Cat, now doubting himself, sunk into the grass and growled. "You're bluffing," he repeated, half yowl, half beg.

The Rook flew around in a large loop before landing heavily on his uninjured legs behind Michael. Up close, the unknown words were making the hairs on the back of his neck stand up. Something was jarring and inherently *wrong* about them. Without wanting to, Michael felt faint, vision growing blurry. He held his good hand out to steady himself, finding his fingers in the feathers on the Rook's shoulder.

It was something like Latin, something dead and not used, but much more guttural and wild than any human language, Michael knew. He tried not to concentrate on listening, but with the Rook right beside him, it was too hard. The words had power, and it wasn't the good kind.

Michael felt his knees buckle as the Rook's voice rose. The Cat was next to the Wolf at that point, fur literally standing on end, both of them shaking. Just as Michael fell, the two turned and bolted, as if that was the trigger for their flight.

He was barely aware of what happened after that. The Rook immediately stopped talking in that horrible, dead language and rose to his hind legs, albeit with a slight limp. He tore off his ram skull and tossed it to the ground, kneeling beside Michael.

"*This* is why I don't sleep," the Rook told him.

Michael awoke the next morning feeling weak and feverish. The Rook had no sympathy whatsoever for him. It wasn't as if he had much, anyway, but it would have been a little nice to get some. Especially since Michael only felt terrible because of the Rook. Plus there was the matter of his broken arm and wrist, which were also the Rook's fault.

"If I didn't cause it, it's not my fault." That was the Rook's stubborn view on Michael's list of grievances.

The boy had tried ignoring the Rook, just out of spite, but that unfortunately only added to said list. "Some help you are!" he ended up snapping.

"*Excuse* me? Need I remind you who saved you from the two hunters?" the Rook asked incredulously, eyebrows raised.

"You nearly killed me in the process!" He wasn't sure how, but he was sure of that fact. Whatever the Rook had been doing had scared the Wolf and Cat badly enough that they'd rather run than face it. Not to mention how badly Michael felt afterward. It was as if a piece of his soul had been ripped out.

"Maybe. I don't know about that one." The Rook relaxed against a tree, wings folded casually over his shoulders like the cloak he often wore. "I'm serious!" he said in respond to Michael's flat glare. "It's only supposed to kill whoever can understand it. Lethal to us, not so much to humans."

"It sure didn't feel that way."

"I don't know, then. I haven't had to resort to it often to kill humans." The Rook shrugged, feathers ruffling. "...You know I'd never intentionally hurt you, Michael." The afterthought was too quiet, too serious.

"I'm trying to hate you right now. Don't pull that."

"Are you talking back to me?"

"No."

The broken bones did pose a problem, however. Michael had been injured in a lot of ways a lot of different times— bruised, scratched, scraped, hit, kicked, dropped, burned—but he hadn't yet broken a bone. Especially not one as serious as his arm, which he regularly needed. Michael immediately saw the solution, even if the Rook wouldn't like it: go to a human hospital. Doctors would fix him up, and as long as he stayed polite (but essentially silent), he wouldn't be discovered. Four years, malnutrition, physical abuse, and a changed hair color helped.

Surprisingly, however, the Rook agreed. "My leg hurts, so maybe they could—"

"Doctors might notice you aren't breathing."

"...Don't interrupt me, Michael," he said in a low voice, black eyes gleaming.

"...It still wouldn't work," he mumbled, eyes downcast. "Doctors are smart. They would figure out you're not human in a heartbeat."

"I have one of those, at least," the Rook huffed, crossing his arms.

"You also don't regularly eat or sleep, and the Cat said you have hollow bones. Only birds have those. Not anything else."

Michael eventually persuaded the Rook not to try that. And by persuaded, it meant he refused to speak until the Rook gave in. It earned him a few bruises and some blood loss, but it was worth it. Things had been going downhill lately, and the easier they made it on themselves, the better.

The city they went to was a smaller one this time. Michael made sure it was large enough to allow them to get lost in the crowds, though, and that it had an equally large hospital. No one looked twice at a limping man and a boy holding his arm, thankfully. People were always too busy with their own lives to care about others, after all. As usual, Michael was grateful for that.

People might've not cared, but demons sure did. When the hospital was in sight, just down the street, the Rook suddenly stopped and started looking around him again. Michael grit his teeth and stopped too. "...This one's fainter. They're not close." The Rook didn't sound terribly sure of that, however.

"They'll get close, won't they? If you can sense them—can't they do the same?" Michael asked worriedly. There was no way they had caught up that fast, was there? Couldn't be. Things were happening too quickly, though, so he didn't exactly doubt it.

"We can buy time." The Rook started walking again, pushing Michael forward ahead of him.

"Where are we going?"

"To the hospital. You can finish getting fixed before they catch up. They're still not that close."

"It will take too long," he protested, digging in his heels.

"If they come, then I will come get you."

"Where will you be?!" Michael asked in a voice too high for his liking. He didn't fancy being caught alone by those two again. The Rook was his only chance for protection, so he wasn't going to leave willingly.

"Just outside—"

"No!"

Michael stopped fully and turned around. The Rook stared down at him, surprise written in his raised eyebrows and slight frown. "Did you just talk back to me?" he asked curiously, as if he honestly weren't sure.

"If you leave me, they will get me," Michael replied evenly, trying his best to glare at him.

"I won't let them—"

"They got me last time because I was alone, didn't they?!"

"Don't raise your voice to me." The Rook placed his hands on Michael's shoulders warningly. "When you called, I came, didn't I? I won't let them get past me this time."

"...B-But—"

His grip tightened, making him wince. "Don't argue." He tore his gaze from Michael's for a moment, scanning the street. "They're closer, but not that much closer. They're only after *me*, so it's unlikely they'll try going for you again if they find me first. Go hide in one of the human buildings and wait. I'll come get you when I'm done, then we can get you fixed at your hospital, and then we can go."

The absurdity of his plan was all too obvious, but Michael really wasn't in a position to argue. The Rook's claws were digging into his shoulders so hard, he was afraid he was bleeding. The boy was pushed into the nearest door. One look at the Rook made him stay inside; he hadn't acted that scary in a long time. Michael knew not to argue anymore and instead wait out the Rook's stubbornness… or wait out the ensuing fight.

Michael looked around. It appeared to be a bar or a restaurant of some sort. The lighting was dim and the air was smoky, making him squint at the surroundings. He tried not to think about the Rook, the Cat, or the Wolf. The bar-restaurant didn't seem too crowded, although there were a lot of waitresses bustling about. Michael shuffled awkwardly out of the way as one sashayed past with a pair of drinks. Should he sit down to be out of the way? Or should he stay standing by the door to show that he wasn't going to buy anything? Actually, he *was* sort of hungry, so maybe he should—?

"Hey there, cutie. Gonna sit down and order somethin'?" Cutting off his internal debate, one of the waitresses had finally noticed him.

"Um, I'm not sure..." he mumbled, looking down. She was pretty, so it made him shy and feel a little uncomfortable.

"Aw, come on now. Come in and sit awhile," she said lightly with her slight accent. The woman reached down and took his wrist, pulling him forward.

"Who's this?" Suddenly, there were more beautiful women showing curiosity in Michael. They seemed to be fascinated by the fact that he was just trying to stand there and mind his own business. They also weren't quiet or shy when it came to touching him. He was pushed, pulled, hugged, petted and hugged until about four or five of them got him into one of the stools at the bar.

"How old are you?" a very busty blonde asked, leaning forward with a smile.

"F-Fourteen." Oh God. When had *this* happened? And *why* had it happened? Michael stared, red-faced, down at the marble surface of the bar. The waitresses were friendly enough, but this was becoming awkward.

"Oh, you're so *young*," she said in surprise.

"Why're you in a place like this, sweetie?" another asked with a giggle.

"Like you *need* to ask Amber!" the blonde said, a little forcefully. She then returned her attention to Michael. She draped an arm over his shoulders, playing with a lock of dark hair near his ear. Michael stared stoically down. At that point, he would almost rather face the Wolf. At least she had some decency, even if it was a bit violent.

He also got the feeling that this wasn't the typical restaurant.

"I-I think I have to be going," he announced shakily, still not raising his eyes.

"Aww! You scared him *off*, Star!"

"Nice going!"

"Don't leave, stay with us!"

"I really think I should be going," he repeated, though he still made no move to leave. The attention, while embarrassing and slightly annoying, was also kind of… nice. Plus the Rook *had* shoved him in here and made him fend for himself.

"*Oi*! You girls, get your asses back to work!" Suddenly, a boss-looking man started shouting. Most of the women dispersed with nervous, high-pitched giggles. Two were left with Michael: the one across from him at the bar and one sitting next to him on a stool, long legs crossed.

"I got this one," the one sitting next to him told the waitress across from them in a low tone, probably thinking Michael hadn't heard her. She then turned back to him with a dazzling smile. He looked away, having made the mistake of looking up in the first place.

She *was* pretty, he'd readily admit, but she also had the air of knowing too much. That wasn't something he was very comfortable with right then. She flipped her brown hair, tied with a ribbon, over her shoulder and leaned forward, emphasizing her low-cut shirt.

"You seem tense," she told Michael with a bright smile.

"I-I kind of am right now," he admitted, eyes anywhere but down her shirt.

"Why?"

"I shouldn't be here. Probably not. No."

"Why not?" she pouted, winding one arm around Michael's waist to pull herself closer. She hooked one ankle around his leg. He definitely wanted to get out of there. The Rook would never let him live this down, even if it was all *his* fault to begin with. Michael would never forgive him for it, either.

"I have to meet someone." He tried to push himself to his feet, but she reached out to make him stay—and grabbed his broken arm. He flinched back and tried not to growl in pain. He met her surprised eyes. "I have to go," he said firmly, arm still hurting.

"Why do you have to leave so soon? Is that Rook really that important to you?" she whined, pushing out her bottom lip. Michael shook his head—and then realized exactly what she had said.

He stared at her, mouth agape. She beamed back at him, tilting her head slightly to the side. Keeping his blue eyes on her, he turned towards the front of the restaurant, hoping the Rook was still out there. "Ro—"

Immediately, she was standing in front of him, hand clapped over his mouth. Her sharp nails gleamed even in the dim light. "No, no no no. Let's not do that, not yet," she breathed in his ear. "You and I are going to leave together, and you are *not* going to call that Rook. If you cause a scene, this will not end prettily. And if I lose my job here, I will *not* be happy."

Michael nodded mutely, breaking out in a cold sweat.

He *knew* they shouldn't have split up.

Michael and his captor went out the back entrance. She had her arm around his shoulders and was all smiles, telling her boss that she was going on break. He accepted it as an answer and ignored the pleading look Michael sent him.

Once outside, she let go of him. He almost relaxed, until she whirled around and slammed him against the brick wall, holding him with her arm across his chest. "You *reek* of the Rook. Doesn't that bird know anything?" she said sourly, wrinkling her nose in disgust.

"Who are you?" Michael had to ask. She was not the Cat or the Wolf. The Rook had been vague when describing his species and how many there were, but it sure would have been nice to know that there were *others* hunting him.

"I'm the Rabbit. And you are?" she asked politely. He had no idea what to make of her civility.

"Uh—Michael."

"You're the Rook's new plaything, huh?" The Rabbit held him out from her, looking him up and down appraisingly. She then leaned in close again, reaching up with her free hand to curl a lock of his black hair around her finger. "...You're nothing like his last one..." she murmured to herself.

"If you're looking for him—"

"Are you *kidding*?! I don't want him anywhere *near* me!" she squeaked, snapping back to attention. She took a breath— apparently, she was used to the process, unlike the Rook—and calmed herself. "I'm not stupid enough to get in the middle of *that* fight."

"Then why did you kidnap me?"

The Rabbit looked at him contemplatively for a moment. "...You're injured. The Rook did that to you?"

"The Wolf did."

She hissed. "Of course she did. She never *did* care much about others." He considered it comforting that she wasn't on their side, even if she wasn't on the Rook's, either. A neutral party was more than he had been hoping for earlier.

"She's chasing us, with the Cat. We're trying to get away. Can you help us?"

"I told you, I'm not getting anywhere near that fight of theirs!" she replied, shaking her head. Now, too late, he noticed how her chocolate hair was tied into two plaits near her ears, looking a whole lot like rabbit ears.

"Then what are you—"

"You're *cute*, Michael. Don't you want to get away from that nasty Rook? He doesn't care for you, I can assure you." Like Michael needed a lot of convincing of that fact. His thought process promptly shut down, however, when the Rabbit pressed her body up against his. "I can get you away from him; come with me instead."

"I-I—" He hadn't been so inarticulate since the Rook had taken Tuesday away. These were very different situations, even if that didn't make him feel too much better about the current one.

"You can't possibly be attached to him. Come with me, Michael, and I'll show you a good time. Not all of us are so cruel to humans," she whispered, pushing her breasts up against his chest. The Rabbit nuzzled into the crook of his neck. "I could be kind to you, Michael."

Words were beyond him at that point.

At least, all but one. "Rook!"

The Rabbit's claws dug into his wrists and she reared back, narrowing her eyes. "How could you—?!" She didn't get to finish, because Michael's supernatural bodyguard showed up at that point. Michael hadn't expected him to actually appear, but the Wolf had been right in the fact that he seemed to when called.

"What are you *doing*?!" The Rook didn't sound too happy. Though really, none of them were too happy in the current situation.

"If you touch me, I will rip his hands off," the Rabbit said, glaring at the brick wall above Michael's shoulder. To emphasize her point, she tightened her grip on his wrists until the blood ran freely down both their arms. He cringed when she did; she noticed. She loosened her grip slightly on his injured arm, eyes softening as she looked away.

Michael let out a breath he hadn't known he'd been holding. He tore his gaze away from the Rabbit and instead looked at the Rook standing across the alley. He looked as angry as he'd ever seen him, even when he'd hit Michael or when he had been fighting the Cat and Wolf.

"Let him go. He's mine," the Rook snapped.

"Make me," the Rabbit taunted back, turning to give him a smirk. He growled and took a step forward. She pressed up against Michael again—much to his irritation—and tensed once more. "Take one more step and your little Michael will bleed to death."

The Rook responded by leaping at them, wings bursting from his shoulders for the extra surge of speed he needed. The Rabbit screamed and suddenly, Michael was in her arms, down the alley. She clung to him like one would a doll, glaring balefully over his mop of black hair at the Rook.

"You're an idiot, Rook! You ca—can't catch me, and *why* did you have to bring your wings out?! You'll only get spotted!" she shouted, pulling Michael closer to her.

"*I'll* get spotted? You're the one prancing around at that speed of yours!" He flexed his wings and crouched down for another leap. The Rabbit backed up a step, shifting Michael in her arms so she could hold one hand up to stop him with.

"If you cause a panic, I'll run away and you'll never find us!" Michael couldn't help but wonder why she hadn't done that already, then. Not that he was complaining.

"Try it, bun, and I will kill you when I catch up to you! I'll take those long ears of yours and wrap them around your throat and will make you *wish* I'll kill you quickly. I'll have you *begging* for death!" he crowed, stalking towards them, wings still tensed for flight. "Hand him over. He's mine."

"N-No he's not!" the Rabbit retorted. Michael could feel her shaking and she hugged him even more tightly. "You abuse him and can't understand how good it is to have a human! You don't value him!"

"Are you kidding me? Michael's my angel!" The Rook laughed harshly, advancing. The Rabbit darted farther down the alley, pulling the boy along with her once more. "Give him back!"

"No!"

"Now, Rabbit!"

"No!"

The Rabbit sped past the Rook, back towards the door they had come out of. This time, when she stopped, Michael was starting to feel sick. The one-sided high-speed chase was beginning to get to his stomach.

His mind was in a similar condition; he didn't know whether to trust the Rabbit and try to get away from the Rook, or go back to the Rook like he normally would. Which would be the lesser of the evils? He really didn't know. At least the Rook had never threatened to tear his hands off.

"You scared of makin' a scene, bun? Don't want to scare off all of your little human prey?" the Rook asked evilly, staring pointedly down the alley to where multitudes of people passed by ignorantly. "How many of them are you willing to lose before you let go of mine?"

"I don't care about those—just don't be stupid about this! If the humans spot us, you know the Cat and Wolf will immediately be all over this." Her voice was calm and level, even if she was still shaking. He didn't know if she was really that scared of the Rook or if it was something else, and that worried him.

The Rook stopped advancing and stared hard at her.

She broke out into a pretty little smile. "Humans are very good at panicking, Rook. It's taken me decades to get to the point where I'm invisible among them. Even the two hunters couldn't find me. But *you*, on the other hand... Well, you stand out in a crowd. Do you really want to drag poor little Michael around with you as you try to stay one step ahead of them? Michael needs humanity, but humanity will notice you, Rook. He can't stay with you. Are you really going to hurt him like this?"

"Yes, I am," the Rook replied smoothly without missing a beat. Michael sighed. The Rabbit was too naïve about their relationship, especially if she honestly thought that that would work.

"You... You really don't value what you've got, do you?!" the Rabbit exclaimed viciously. The Rook merely gave her a bored glare. "You—You had a lot, you know! Not everyone was as lucky as you were! But then you just had to take *more*, didn't you?! You had to go after the Ram and take his head!"

"What happened between us is none of your concern—"

"None of my concern?! You have half the world in chaos because of what you did!" she shrieked, loosening her hold on Michael in order to point angrily at the Rook. "Twice I've had to talk my way out of going back there!"

"At least you *can* go back there!" he snarled, suddenly enraged. Wings flapping in agitation behind him, he paced back and forth in front of them, continuing, "Do you know how hard it is to try to live amongst these humans?! We all can't be whores like you can, bun! Do you know what I *lost* by doing that?! You couldn't, could you!"

"Don't make me laugh! You just got greedy, you stupid bird, you saw something shiny and had to go for it—"

"Don't pretend like you know what went on between that Ram and I—"

"I don't have to pretend, all the world knows what you did—"

"I bet you don't know half of what really happened—"

"You *stole* his *head*, ripped it clean off—"

The Rabbit finally dropped Michael altogether. He hit the ground rather hard, not expecting it, and made a mad dash for the door. He didn't care who won the argument or the fight; he didn't want to be caught in another one. He slammed the door shut behind him before either of them noticed he was missing.

Inside, several people looked up as he leaned against the back door, chest heaving and arm hurting. Michael was intensely aware of the fact that he was sweaty and bleeding, too. He just ducked his head and wove his way towards the front of the restaurant. He passed the boss, who looked mildly annoyed, probably at the fact that his employee hadn't returned yet.

Michael made it all the way outside before the two fighting demons he left behind caught back up.

The Rabbit darted out into the street, screaming bloody murder. The Rook chased after her, lip curled in a silent snarl as he tried to catch up to her. People immediately took notice of the black wings. Michael groaned and tried to pretend he didn't know either of them.

"You got me *fired*, you stupid, stupid bird! I liked this job! I am going to kill you!" the Rabbit screeched, tackling the Rook at full speed. He went down onto the asphalt of the street. He wiped the blood from his chin and glowered at her, ignoring the traffic veering around him.

"You deserved it, whore! You decided to mess with Michael for no good reason and this is what you get! Don't think you can get away with that, either—I'll tear your head clean off your body if that's what it takes to drive the message home! Ask the Ram how much he liked that!" he yelled, voice hoarse. He threw his arms open wide, wings stretching to mirror the action. Michael saw people all around them gasp and back up, unaware that they had really been *real*.

"You're causing a scene!" the Rabbit screamed, running at him again. The Rook sidestepped her and she managed to run right into his outstretched arm. He caught her under the chin and she hit the ground with a nasty crack. The Rook was immediately on top of her, taking her head in his hand and slamming it against the ground.

"*I'm*—" thud "—the one—" thud "—making a—" *crack* "—scene?!" he shouted at her. The Rabbit didn't reply. People started screaming when they noticed the pool of blood underneath her head. Michael clamped a hand over his mouth to stop himself from either screaming along with them or throwing up. The Rook unsteadily got back to his feet, grinning down at her. "What now, bun?!"

"I-I say you're a terribly stupid bird," the Rabbit answered, hooking her arm around his ankle and pulling him down to the ground. Now their positions were reversed, although she was bleeding from far too many places to be normal—or human. Michael noticed he was the only one watching anymore. Everyone else had ran away to a safer distance, peering out of windows and from around corners.

He also noticed the cameras.

Michael jumped when he did; cameras equaled evidence which equaled identification which equaled *not good*. He covered his face as best he could with one hand, running out to the fighting pair. "G-Guys! Rook, Rabbit, stop this!"

The Rabbit looked up at him, hands locked around the Rook's throat. "What is it, Michael?" she asked with a dazzling smile, ignoring the blood dripping down her lips.

"You didn't want to cause a scene, right? Well—you are," he said firmly, hoping to God that the demons listened to him for once.

The Rabbit looked around, growing pale. She hesitantly released her grasp on the Rook. He winced and sat up, shoving her off him. "What are you doing, Michael?"

"I'm making sure the police don't get involved and capture us all!" he retorted with a bravado he wasn't feeling. "If we get captured, then it means—"

"Off with his head!" the Rook muttered with a smirk.

"No, it means that *we'll* get captured, too," the Rabbit whispered fearfully. The Rook rolled his eyes. "I'm serious! If they can catch us, they will find out about us and they'll dissect us and they'll try to do all sorts of nasty things to us!"

"We'll just kill 'em all," he said as he got up to his feet, dusting off his pants. "Come on, Michael, unless you want all of these people to die."

"*I* was the one telling *you* to leave!" he hissed, though it earned him a smack to the back of the head.

Ignoring the cameras and people all around them, the Rook stretched his arms and wings, then scooped up Michael, and flew off. Michael glanced back down just in time to see the Rabbit dart off, only a blur of motion.

That night, she reappeared at the edges of their firelight. She didn't speak or announce her presence, even if the two knew

107

she was there, and instead flickered around them like the flames in front of them.

And that was how Michael came to be haunted by a second monster.

CHAPTER SEVEN

The Fingers Point Right **Back At You**

"Get out of the shadows. You're not stealthy." That was all the beckoning the Rabbit needed. She stood across from them, keeping the fire in between herself and the Rook. Michael glared at her from where he was bandaging up his wrists. It was hard to do considering one of them was still broken.

"You got me fired." She even had the gall to accuse them. Or probably just the Rook, since that was who she was clearly wishing a horrible death upon.

"You're the one who started the scene," he replied flippantly, shrugging.

The Rook then turned his attention solely to Michael, only to further annoy the Rabbit. She silently fumed as he took the bandages from the boy and wrapped up both arms for him. In other circumstances, Michael would have been touched and alarmed by the gesture, but it was only too obvious what the Rook's motives were, so he ignored the act. "...I still have a broken arm, you know," he muttered under his breath, wincing as the Rook pulled a bit too tightly on it.

"I'll fix it for you later, alright?" he replied with a bright, cheery smile. Michael had to look away, lest he have nightmares about it.

"...Okay..."

"Stop ignoring me!" the Rabbit demanded, crossing her arms over her chest. Michael glanced at her, scowling. The Rook continued blatantly ignoring her. She huffed and darted over to plop down next to Michael, rabbit-hair flying. She immediately wrapped her arms around his waist and set her head on his shoulder before either he or the Rook could react. "*Michael* won't ignore me. He's so much better than you are."

"Get off," both Michael and the Rook said in unison. She

dug her nails into Michael's side with a smirk, making him flinch and bite his tongue to prevent any sounds. The Rook noticed this and reached over to grab her, but she darted off, stopping on the other side of the fire again.

"You two got me fired, so I'm going to come with you now," she told them primly, all business.

"Like hell," the Rook replied, lifting Michael's arm to look at his side. It was all he could do to restrain himself from snatching his limb back. "You're not bleeding. I think you're getting better at this."

"At not bleeding?"

"Stop ignoring me! I'm staying with you guys and there's nothing you can do but accept that fact! So stop it." The Rabbit sat down and crossed her arms over her chest once more.

"You're making an awful lot of assumptions, bun." The Rook finally turned and looked at her with an icy glare. She twitched and ducked down, however slightly, which made him lean back triumphantly. "You'll only get in the way. We don't want or need you around."

"The Cat and Wolf are still tracking you. I can help you get them off your tail," she offered. The Rook contemplated this and watched her with a hooded gaze. "I'm good at hiding myself. I had been working that job for *years* before you two came along and ruined it for me. No one's ever found me if I didn't want to be found."

"No one's *looking* for you."

"I could help, if only a little bit. For starters, the problem with Michael." She nodded towards the black-haired boy. He replied by sticking his tongue out at her. She mimicked him until the Rook threw a rock at her head. "Hey! Do you want my help or not?!"

"Don't need it, don't want it," he answered airily, tossing

another from hand to hand as a warning. "Get out of here, bun. Go whore yourself out to some other human city."

"I knew Michael was yours before I even saw him," she stated coldly. Michael felt the chill from her words; it had been true. She had mentioned the Rook so easily, so calmly, and had singled him out from the start...

"It's true," he said quietly, cutting across the Rook's rude reply. The man scrutinized him, then turned back to the Rabbit, and then back again. "She asked me about you." Now it was her turn to lean back triumphantly.

"...How?" he asked after a pause.

"He smells just like you. He smells more like you than *you* do," she said with a wide smirk that showed her teeth. The Rabbit flipped one of her plaits over her shoulder and tilted her head to one side with that same grin. "It's all too easy to sniff out a human who's been with a demon, especially one that's as been with one for as long as you two have been together. How long has that been, by the way?"

"Too long," Michael said with a sigh. The Rook snorted and hit him upside the head.

"He doesn't smell any differently than he normally does," the Rook protested, grabbing Michael around the shoulders and pulling him practically into his lap. Just to make his point, he sniffed his hair, too.

"You can't smell your own scent, you stupid bird."

"I think I'd notice if—"

"*That's* how the two trackers are following you, I can guarantee it. You can hide your own smell easily enough in most cases—masquerading as a human helps with that—but Michael can't. You'll need my help if you ever want to get rid of the Cat and Wolf."

"Oh, I'll get rid of them next time I see them. How's that

for a guarantee?"

"You almost killed me last time, too," Michael added unhelpfully. The Rabbit frowned and nodded at the Rook.

"See? It'd be easier to just hide from them."

"It's not like they'll give up."

"If you're hiding, then you have the element of surprise. You could turn the tables and kill them at your leisure."

"I could kill them anyway—"

"Not without putting Michael's life in danger. Do you *really* want to do that?"

"Of course not!"

Strangely, it was surprisingly easy to fall asleep on the Rook's shoulder listening to them bicker. Michael was tired enough as it is, and not only from the horribly eventful day. His injuries were getting to him, too.

The next morning when he awoke, the Rabbit was still alive and hadn't left, so he assumed she'd be staying with them. Michael was torn about this development. On one hand, it meant he could potentially have an ally against the Rook and his incessant abuse. On the other, he already knew a bit of how the Rabbit acted and didn't want to get anywhere near her. Walking the tightrope between them put him on edge.

What put him even more on edge was when she dragged Michael over to the Rook and demanded, "Fix him."

"Why?"

"Fix his arms! Now, Rook."

"Why?" he repeated blandly. Michael very much would have liked to know that as well.

"Because if you don't, I will go tell the Cat and Wolf where you are," she threatened, narrowing her eyes. She was nowhere *near* as scary as the Rook, but she was still intimidating in her own right.

"Do that and I'll kill you where you stand." He didn't sound amused with the threat, but at least he was giving her his full attention now. "You're too much of a coward to do that, anyway."

"I take offense to that!"

"Go ahead and take it all you want." The indifference was back again. Michael couldn't help but roll his eyes. If *this* was how they were going to act, maybe he didn't have as much to worry about as he'd thought.

"Fix him, Rook! Or else I'll take him back to the city and do it myself!" she said in a high voice, hands tight on Michael's shoulders. Something about that or its potential consequences must've given the Rook something to think about, because he hauled Michael off after that.

He instructed him to sit on a half-dead fallen tree. Michael did so, mostly because it was one of the safer things the Rook had told him to do in the course of their association. The man disappeared with the beginnings of his muttering, sending shivers down his spine.

It took awhile, but eventually he came back. There was a bit of blood on his hands, but otherwise, he was surprisingly clean. Michael figured he'd been out killing, and was proven correct with the Rook placed his hands on his arms. He winced a bit at the pressure, but soon enough, they were feeling much better. He wasn't sure if his arm or wrist were actually *healed*, but they didn't hurt, so he wasn't complaining.

"...Thank you," he mumbled after a silence. He wasn't sure about the implication that the Rook could have healed him of any of his injuries at any time, though, and simply didn't.

"It wasn't a human life this time, but I still killed for you," the Rook responded in an equally quiet tone.

"Are you saying you're against killing for me?" Michael

114

asked. He had meant the question to be bitter and slightly rhetorical, but instead, it came out as an actual *question*.

"You know I'm not," he replied with a sharp grin.

Hastily changing the subject, the boy asked, "H-How do you do that, anyway?"

"I steal other lives and give them to you. Some of it gets lost in the process, of course, but that's essentially what it is." The Rook seemed fine with the changed subject; happy, even, to be explaining that. Of course, the dark topic he was covering was at odd with his general mood. "It's how I usually kill. Or, actually, how I was designed to kill."

"Instead you like to fight."

"Of course. There's something so much more satisfying about crunching bone in your hands and spilling blood," he replied with a wistful sigh.

Michael was starting to get seriously creeped out, so he didn't complain when the Rabbit came to fetch him at that point. "Are you two *done* here?" She put her hands on her hips and drummed her fingers against her skin.

"...What the hell are you wearing," the Rook asked. It was not an inquiry, since they were probably both too shocked to properly ask anything.

The Rabbit looked down at herself. She was only in her underwear—if what she was wearing even qualified. It hardly covered anything and Michael could feel his face heat up just looking. She looked back up at them and grinned, cupping her hands under her breasts to show them off. At that point, Michael had to look away.

"You're wearing human stuff," the Rook added in that same shell-shocked tone. "...You're wearing human whore stuff. What the *hell*, bun?!" It really didn't surprise Michael that *that* was what the Rook chose to be offended by.

115

"I'm taking Michael," she replied delicately when she darted over to where they were and took Michael's now uninjured arm, "And we are going to go wash all of this Rook stink off of him. You naturally can't come since that would be highly counterproductive."

"I'm not going anywhere with you!" Michael snapped, still blushing madly. The Rook noticed this and growled at the Rabbit.

"Let go of him or you'll lose the hand."

"I'm trying to *help*," she objected, glaring at the Rook. Of course, he glared right back. "Do you want those hunters to find us or not?"

"One bath is *not* going to do anything!"

"You're right, but it's the first step. This is the least you could do for getting me fired!"

"I'm not letting you have Michael!"

"Just for a little while!"

"I'm not an object to be argued about!" Michael exclaimed, wrenching his arms away from both of them. He stood up before the Rook could hit him, and whirled around to face them. "I'll go take a bath on my *own* if that's what I need."

"Aww—"

"Shut up, whore," the Rook deadpanned, hitting her instead of Michael for once.

It just so happened to end up that the Rabbit crashed his swim in the nearest river, anyway. In her defense, it seemed to be (mostly) accidental. The Rook had been chasing her and she ran right off of the bank and nearly landed on Michael. The Rook soon followed, so he was not happy with the idea of a bath by the time they were done picking the wet feathers off everyone.

"From now on, no more wings near water," Michael sighed, running his fingers through the Rabbit's hair to get all of them out.

"Are you giving me an order?" the Rook asked crossly. He was angrier at the fact that he was dripping wet than actually at Michael, however.

"In this case, he is, and I second the motion," the Rabbit responded for him. "And maybe I'll admit that a bath might not have been the best way to go about this. But luckily for the stupid bird, I have a better plan."

The Rook rolled his eyes, pulling his wet wings closer around himself. "*Great.* Another harebrained scheme."

"Did you just make a *pun*?" she asked, sounding thoroughly insulted by the very thought.

"So what if I did, bun? What are you going to do about it, run away again? It's all you're good for, anyway."

Michael stayed out of it and finished pulling the feathers out of her hair. He pretended to busy himself drying his hair, mostly because he didn't want to get near either of them. The Rook seemed actually angry, and the Rabbit really wasn't helping things.

"I'll just take Michael and leave, then!"

"I will kill you."

Okay, maybe staying out of it wasn't the best option. Glancing up from toweling off his hair with his shirt, he asked dully, "What was this plan of yours?"

She brightened at being addressed by him. "We move back to the city!"

The Rook and Michael stared at her incredulously. She couldn't have known about the first time they tried returning to civilization, but she had been there for the second one. Humanity and the Rook simply didn't mesh well.

"Don't look at me that way—this is actually a smart move, trust me." She held up her hands, cutting off any interruptions preemptively. "Not only will this give us a suitable cover and means of living properly, it will help with your tracking problem. If Michael is exposed to humans again, he'll slowly start to lose your scent. You'll start to smell less like yourself, too. If we can stay with humans long enough, not even the Wolf will be able to sniff you two out."

"They'll sniff us out before that happens, though. What then?" Michael asked. It did make a bit of sense, though, and would explain how she was able to stay under the radar for so long. Plus, unlike the Rook, the Rabbit seemed to have more than an ounce of sense about humans, even if that sense was a little disturbing.

"We city-hop until they stop catching up to us. Plus, cities are fairly small when it comes to actual area. If we stay there for awhile, the whole place will smell faintly of you; that'll help throw them off."

"*This* is how you live among them for so long?" the Rook asked with a raised eyebrow.

"Yes, it is. I can tell you it works, too, so don't give me that sort of look," she answered him with a wrinkled nose. "We might have to move a couple times, but it will help in the long run."

"I can't hold a job. Neither can the Rook," Michael pointed out. He didn't fancy having either of them mug innocent people for cash, either.

"I can!" she beamed. "Plus I still have some money leftover from before. I tell you, I'm good at being human. I have a bank account and *everything*." She was inordinately proud of this fact.

As neither the Rook nor Michael wanted to think too much about her choice of a job, they blindly agreed and allowed her to pick the next place to live. It was to the southwest of where they were, and a fair distance away, which would hopefully serve to keep the two trackers away from them for a little bit longer.

The Rabbit, true to her word, set up everything for them. She made it to the city before they did and managed to secure living quarters and a job for herself. If Michael hadn't known what that entailed, he would have been impressed.

He was impressed, though, at what sort of place she came up with to live in. She really must have had a fair amount of money stored up, because it was *nice*. The Rabbit had gotten them a penthouse apartment, a huge, amazing one. Even the Rook was a bit awed at the floor to ceiling windows in several of the rooms, and could only press his hands and face up against the glass and stare out for the longest time. (Michael was busy bouncing on one of the beds during that.)

"See, Michael? I could treat you well," the Rabbit said, standing near the doorway with a small, shy smile. Michael flopped down onto the bed, grinning at the ceiling.

"Don't you have work to get to?" the Rook asked before he could reply. Michael frowned; the Rabbit had just done something really nice for them, and the Rook was being rude, as usual.

The days passed with the Rook's nearly constant rudeness, Michael's cautious excitement, and the Rabbit's smiles and hesitance to get near either of them. It was obvious why she was suddenly keeping her distance: the Rook. All three of them living in such close proximity only made the two snap at each other more and more often, and more of those encounters ended up with the Rook as a very clear winner.

Michael eventually came to dislike that apartment more and more because of it. When the Rook and Rabbit fought, he would either be literally caught in the middle, be somehow the cause of it, or have to suffer the consequences when a very angry Rook came to find him. The Rook never did break any bones—it almost seemed as if he was taking special care not to—but he got more and more creative in his other methods of abuse.

More than once, Michael found the Rabbit staring at him from the bathroom door as he washed the blood off in the sink. He usually ignored her; it was safer to ignore her than risk the Rook knowing he had spoken to her. He sometimes abstractly wondered if he was getting attached or not to the Rabbit, and if the Rook really was just spiteful or if he was trying to take preventive measures.

After two weeks, Michael spoke to her alone for the first time since they had moved. "Why are you helping us?" He didn't look at her, and instead stared at his reflection in the mirror before him. A boy too old for his broken body stared resentfully back at him, watery blood dripping down his chin from the nosebleed he'd just managed to stop.

"I don't fancy helping the ungrateful Rook. I'm helping *you*, Michael," she replied softly, hands clenched tightly on the frame of the door. The Rabbit glanced back over her shoulder, as if to make sure they were alone.

"Why?" he had to know.

"The Rook doesn't value you as a human."

"And you do?" Michael looked away, trying to fight a sarcastic smile. He knew how demons 'valued' humans. They valued them beaten and bloody and ruined. The Rabbit was no exception; she just did her damage in a more passive way.

She leaned her head against the doorframe, bangs nearly obscuring her eyes. They almost looked red in the half-light. "Of course I do. How could you think I don't? Look at all I've done for you…" she murmured.

Michael tore his gaze away from her reflection and concentrated on washing the rest of the red off his face. "You're just like the Rook," he told her. "You're kind in the name of cruelty."

She drew back from the door, visibly bristling. The Rabbit curled her lip and tightened her grip on the wood, nails digging into it. "...How *could* you even say such a thing?! I am nothing like that Rook, that selfish, brutal, spiteful bird!"

Before he could react, she was in front of him, leaning over him and pinning his wrists over his head. "Wha—"

"You can't *imagine* what I've been put through to get you two here! I've kept you safe from the hunters and *this* is how you repay me?!" she hissed, leaning down until their noses brushed. Michael sucked in a breath. The Rabbit narrowed her eyes. "That Rook has gotten it so easy, and I have to work my tail off just to get men to *look* at me. Why don't you like me, Michael?! Is it because I'm not pretty enough for you? I can make a new body, I can suit you, I could be kind to you! I am so much better than that Rook—and why can't you see that?!"

"G-Get off of me," he ground out, trying to get his arms away from her. No such luck. She pressed down on him, bending him over backwards on the counter. Michael growled at her and struggled, but it only made the edge of the sink press painfully into his back. He bit his lip and tried again to push her off, but she just forced him back down against the sink. Human body or not, she was stronger than he was, and they both knew it. "Get off—!"

"I could turn you in to the Cat and Wolf right now if I wanted," she whispered, digging her nails into his hands. Her breath tickled against his face. "Do you think they would have any pity or patience this time around?"

"Roo—" The Rabbit crushed her lips against his, cutting him off from finishing the call. It was hardly a kiss; she was merely shutting him up. At least this time. She didn't let him go, however, and merely pushed herself against him until he was just about lying horizontally on the sink's counter. Michael opened his mouth against hers and bit down on her lip. He immediately tasted blood and she drew back with a snarl.

He didn't have the chance to speak, however, as she soon returned the favor. He gasped as she nearly bit through his lip. The Rabbit grinned against his mouth; he took the change as an opportunity to spit a mouthful of blood at her.

"Let's not play that way, Michael," she breathed, moving her hands. His freed arms immediately went down to support himself, trying to push himself up off of the counter. Hers went to his hair, yanking his head back. She contemplated his bared throat for a moment before telling him casually, "I may not be the Wolf, but I could easily rip your throat out with my teeth right now."

"Do it," he dared, "And the Rook will kill you for it. You don't want to die. I can tell." It was true. Michael could tell effortlessly who had a death wish and who did not, and she most certainly didn't. Michael glanced back over her shoulder, past her, but the grin with the bloody teeth was only for her.

She leaned in close again, red lips brushing against red lips. "He'd have to catch me—"

"You're already caught," Michael whispered.

"Bun, what have you been doing?" the Rook asked calmly from above them. Horrified, the Rabbit turned to look up at him, brown eyes wide. The boy still in her grasp could feel her shaking. Ever so calmly, the Rook tilted his head to one side, staring hard at them both with his black eyes. "It looks almost as if you've been hurting Michael."

"If you do anything—" she started, voice rising to a hushed, breathy shriek.

The Rook immediately had her by the neck, wrenching her

away from Michael and throwing her against the wall. Michael sat up and massaged his back, watching with a hooded expression. For once, he wouldn't mind it when they fought. In fact, he felt relieved that the Rook had arrived when he had.

"You little whore. Do you really think you could get away with trying to steal what's *mine*?"

"Let go of me! Now, let go!"

"Not until I've beat it through your thick *skull* what's mine is mine and you can't have him!" The emphasis he placed on the word 'skull' made her stop struggling at once, instead staring at him in nothing short of sheer terror.

"Y-You wouldn't dare."

"Are you really in a mood to try me right now, bun?!" the Rook shouted, grabbing a fistful of her hair and slamming her head against the wall. Michael looked away; maybe he wouldn't like this fight, after all. It was starting to make him uncomfortable, and while the Rabbit certainly had overstepped her bounds, he didn't exactly want to see her brutally murdered for it.

The Rabbit looked past the Rook and locked eyes with Michael when he glanced back. "Michael, please," she begged, sensing the opening. "Please don't let him do this. I've helped you, haven't I? Please, I'm sorry, I'll never do it again, just please—"

"Stop talking to him!" The Rook smashed her head against the wall again, grinning when he was rewarded with a loud cracking sound. The grin immediately vanished, however, when he saw that it was the wall, not her head, that had cracked. There was a bloody smear left on it, however.

"Please, don't let him do this," the Rabbit pleaded, words starting to slur. Her eyes were bright, tears beginning to leak out at the corners. The mascara and eyeliner she had put on earlier started to run along with them down her cheeks; that was what did it for Michael.

"Let her go," he muttered, sliding down from the sink.

"What?" The Rook turned his head so sharply it was a wonder it didn't snap his neck. "What are you talking about?" Michael ignored the missing threat.

"Let her go, Rook," he repeated, a bit louder. The Rabbit sobbed in relief.

"Why would I do that?! Did you forget what she was just *doing*—?!"

"No, I didn't! But let her go!" Michael was nearly in tears now, too, seeing the brown hair and brown eyes and black running down the cheeks red with panic. It was like he was back on the island, hearing Tuesday sob to him over her lost future, her lost life. He was ten again, the Rook was killing another pretty brunette, he was losing control and sanity and everything all over again.

It only occurred to Michael later, when he was lying in bed that night trying to forget what had happened, that the Rook had *listened* to him.

CHAPTER EIGHT

Interlude

"I can't believe you two, running off with your tails between your legs. Just because he started singing that song of death—you *know* he wouldn't have done it! Not while he has that boy to watch over."

The Cat and Wolf, heads bowed, took the criticism as best they could. They knew it was true, but fear had won out. They might have been loyal to the cause of capturing the Rook, but it didn't necessarily mean they wanted to die for it. No demon was that selfless.

"If I may..." the Wolf said softly during the pause. She risked a glance upward, ears laid back against her skull. "I think he was fully intent on killing us. I don't believe he thought it would kill the boy."

"...Why do you say that?" The words were curious, if cautious.

"He wasn't bluffing, that I know. But he must not have thought that speaking in a non-human language would have affected him."

"..." He stared hard at the two in front of him for a while, then leaned back with a sigh. "That stupid bird. Of course he wouldn't worry about that until after the fact. He never *was* one to plan ahead."

The Wolf didn't reply, knowing it wasn't her place to.

"Find him again, and this time, *capture* him. Don't come back here again without the Rook. If you need help, ask the Deer or the Snake. I'll tell them to assist you."

The two nodded and left. They barely got out of the way in time, however, as the Snake barged past, dragging an immobile Dolphin. The Cat glanced at the Wolf, jerking his skull towards them. "This could be important," he said quietly. The Wolf nodded slowly. The two turned back and silently crept back until they were in hearing range.

They might not have specialized like any of the others, but both of them had been gifted with a plethora of above average skills, including their hearing. That was why they were the best hunters anywhere; it was true that individual others could hear better, were stronger, or were faster, but they were better than the standard demon and better in more ways. The Cat and Wolf stealthily hovered at the edge of their hearing range, which was far enough away from any of the others for them to be comfortable.

"I brought you the Dolphin," the Snake announced breathily, voice deceptively light. He dropped the paralyzed Dolphin and curled around her, staring upwards for some sort of approval. None was forthcoming, so he added, "She had seen the Owl."

"...Did she now." There still was no approval, but there was a wicked smile in the words. The Snake coiled his tail around the Dolphin's and nodded.

"I have reason to believe that the Mockingbird is with the Owl. They are trying to find the Rook as well. They are using the Mockingbird for that and are trying to find as many useful demons as they can."

The Wolf bit back a growl. The Owl alone was bad news, especially since she was still trying to contact the Rook, even after he turned traitor. But the Mockingbird was even worse. The Mockingbird wasn't very old, but he was sharp and knew how to use his advantage well. The Wolf herself had met him once.

"Things just got interesting," the Cat purred, turning towards her. The Wolf ignored him.

"Do you know how many the Mockingbird has seen?"

The Snake shook his head in that peculiar way he had, swaying with the movement. "No. We can only know of the Dolphin for sure, and assume the Owl as well."

"Add at least three more to that," he replied with a scowl in his tone. The Snake stared up questioningly at him. "The Ram, the Rook, and the Unicorn."

"…This does not bode well," the reptile murmured. "What are they planning?"

"The Owl is still trying to find the Rook before we do. We won't be able to find out her plan until later, more likely than not, but we cannot worry about that now. If we can just get to the Rook first, it won't matter what she does."

The Wolf turned and wagged her tail once in the Cat's direction as a beckon. He followed her without a question. Neither of them spoke until they were well away from the others, back in the human world and searching for the Rook once more.

"I've met the Mockingbird," the Wolf said without preamble. She stood up on her hind legs and gently took off her skull, shaking her ponytail out behind her. Now human in appearance, she looked at the Cat, who was doing the same. "I know his scent."

"Our mission isn't to find the Mockingbird. It's to find the Rook," the Cat replied with a languid stretch and yawn.

"I'm not into overly ambitious actions, but I would like to know more about this situation. If the Owl is planning something, it will undoubtedly only work out well in the end for her."

"So what? It's a race, then. The Owl can't see the future, so we can't be so defeatist when it comes to her."

"But she has the Mockingbird, and that means she might as well have anyone she chooses."

"It's not like he got anything *good*."

"He's already met the Rook, and that alone should put us on our guard," she reminded him. "The fact that he's seen the Dolphin also puts me on edge."

"And that he saw the Ram doesn't?" the Cat joked, smirking. She glared at him. He looked away, smirk turning into an innocent smile. "Look, the Mockingbird won't be a problem unless he gets into some *serious* trouble."

"I'm sorry if the combination of the Owl, Rook and Dolphin doesn't scare me as it is," she sniffed, turning away from him.

"We only have to worry about this if we actually run into him. If not, then who cares? We only have to deal with the Rook. And to do that, all we have to do is keep hold of that boy of his."

"Bear, Bear, please come out!" the Owl implored, clasping her hands together. She had taken her human form, as it was the least threatening and showed the most goodwill. Beside her, the Mockingbird stayed on guard, flexing his wings and shuffling back and forth anxiously.

The pair stood in front of a massive cave entrance. Inside it was the Bear, though she wasn't coming out.

"Please, Bear! We need your help!" the Owl begged, taking a step towards the cave. There was an immediate answering growl. She backed off again, though the Mockingbird took a step forward protectively.

"...What is it that you want, Owl? Surely you *know* that I won't help you." The Bear appeared at the edge of the darkness, rubbing empty eye sockets with a blunt paw. She yawned. The Owl knew it was all a ruse, made to try to make them leave.

"We need your help with something. Just a little thing. If you'd like, no one will ever know that you helped us," the Owl begged, bowing at the waist. The Bear tilted her head, studying them both.

"…Why do you have the Mockingbird with you, then? You do not bring a tool of war for a peaceful entreaty."

"He is no such thing! The Mockingbird has agreed to help me. He will not fight; neither of us will." It was a promise the Owl fully intended to keep, even if it meant disastrous things down the road. While the Mockingbird could easily fight, especially considering who he had met, she was not cut out for physical fighting.

They were trying to make peace, anyway.

The Bear continued to study them. The Owl knew that she would eventually come around, given the right incentive. "…What is it you need help with? I do not wish to get tangled up in your affairs, but even more so without knowing what exactly it is you're attempting to do," the Bear requested neutrally.

The Owl smiled widely. "We just want to see if we can find the Rook without really finding him."

"…Via a dream? He's not sleeping, I can tell you that," the Bear replied indifferently, rubbing at her eyes again.

"That's why we need your help. You have power over slumber, not just what goes on during it. If you would allow the Mockingbird your power and if we could all work together, I believe we could find the Rook," the Owl informed her. "He will have to sleep soon, I know. This will give us a small window of opportunity, and we have to use it."

The Bear padded forward curiously. "…And why would I let the Mockingbird copy me?"

"We are of peace," she repeated firmly. The Mockingbird took a step towards the Owl, pressing his wing against her side defensively. "We only want the ability to take advantage of that opportunity and talk some sense into that Rook."

"…Well, it *is* nice to see that not everyone is out for the dimwitted bird's blood, I suppose," the Bear allowed.

"If we could get this Rook and Ram business cleared up with little more blood shed, it would right the balance in our world again. Or would you rather see decades more of hide and seek with the Rook and chaos while it goes on?"

"…No. Of course not. It's stressful, trying to keep out of these affairs." The Bear slowly shook her head.

"If we can fix this, then we wouldn't have to deal with staying neutral or be forced to gradually take sides," the Owl said softly. She knew she was winning against the Bear, but until she actually said yes, they couldn't rejoice.

"…What of others? Are you enlisting the aid of others?"

"Not directly." The Owl laid a hand on the Mockingbird's shoulder. The Bear nodded in understanding. "If I wasn't certain that this could boost our chances, I would not ask you to help. As it is, however, I feel that we need you, Bear."

"…And what if someone else finds out about this? I am not the strongest of fighters, especially if the Wolf or Cat is sent. I would undoubtedly die for this cause of yours."

"You could help us and leave, and no one will know but us. Or, if you would feel safer, you may stay with us. No one has found us yet and no one shall in the immediate future. Even if they do—you said so yourself. The Mockingbird is here."

"…How is this reassuring?" the Bear baited. The Owl saw it coming; she knew that the Bear would want some information in exchange for her services. Even if this eventually was leaked (which the Owl doubted), perhaps it would be better to hope intimidation worked instead of power itself.

"Do you remember the Ram and the Rook before this all happened?" the Owl asked mildly.

"…Of course I do," she responded, tilting her head warily.

"The Mockingbird met them shortly before their fight. If that is not reassuring enough, I can give you a full list," the Owl declared. The Bear stayed silent, though out of fright or curiosity, she couldn't tell. "The Wolf, the Unicorn, the Deer, the Otter, the Fox, the Rabbit, and most recently, the Dolphin, he has met them all. This is not including myself, or you, if you choose to join us. Would you rather be against him or with him?" She felt a little low, having to resort to using the Mockingbird as a tool for coercion, especially after all that he had done for her. To try to calm her conscience, the Owl tangled her fingers in his short, fine feathers around the base of his wing. It was all for a good cause.

As always, the Mockingbird stayed silent. He didn't respond to the fact that she was blatantly using him.

The Bear, however, swore and shook her head. "...I cannot believe you, Owl. You say you are of peace—but look at what you're doing."

"I am only trying to fix what the Rook has done."

"...I don't see how you can do that."

"I can't explain it to you, because I don't understand it fully myself. But something will have to happen to make him reconcile with what he's done."

"...Will you bully him into it with the Mockingbird? And do you plan on garnering more weapons for that walking arsenal?"

"I'll admit I would like to find the Phoenix and the Turtle, but more as precautionary measures than for fighting purposes," the Owl mumbled. She was not proud of using the Mockingbird or of using others, but it was necessary if any of this was to end well.

The Bear was silent for a long time. She was clearly staring at the Mockingbird rather than the Owl, thinking hard. "...I think you would create quite the terror," she said at last, "If you ever decided to be anything but a pacifist, Owl."

The Owl just smiled in response to the unspoken question.

The Deer wandered aimlessly around the meadow, trying to enjoy the sunshine and mild weather of the human world. The meadow had been the last place the Rook had been seen, so he had been sent to see if there was anything of value there.

All he could see, though, was high grass and pleasant scenery. It wasn't the sort of place the Rook would ever enjoy.

Of course, there was the matter of that human fawn that the Rook had taken under his wing. The human had been spotted first; the Rook had only come when called. That meant that the meadow was a thing the human enjoyed, not the Rook, but that could potentially mean that it was the human deciding where to go, not the Rook.

The Deer stopped to inspect the tracks that the fight had created. There had also been blood spilt, scaring off most native animals and giving the meadow a slightly unhealthy tinge.

The Deer vanished, reappearing on the outskirts of the nearest human city. The Rook had been initially spotted in a city along with his boy. It would make sense, looking at those facts, if the human was deciding the direction of their travels. But taking into account the Rook's personality and arrogance, there was no way he would allow that.

The Deer sighed. It was too hard to try to figure out a pattern. He could either follow the mental steps of the human or the mental steps of the Rook, but not both of them together. They seemed to travel so haphazardly.

He changed into his human disguise before jumping again. It was his job to search the human cities while the Cat and the

Wolf tried to follow his scent trail. He didn't know *how* he was supposed to search the human cities, unfortunately, and couldn't do more than jump from one to another and see if he could sense the Rook in the immediate area.

The Deer disappeared once more and reappeared in front of an alley. He instinctively appeared in places where his kind had been before, so this puzzled him slightly. Maybe the Rook *was* here—or had been. The Deer didn't notice his presence, so he assumed he wasn't here any longer.

Another city, another story with the same ending: the Rook wasn't there. The Deer continued jumping from city to city, walking along with the humans while he waited for his ability to come back. He couldn't teleport very often, at least not without serious consequences. It allowed him to search the area a bit, though, so it worked well with his mission in this instance.

The days passed quickly when one was searching for a truant demon. The Deer continued searching silently.

He marveled at how humans could stand to live in such close proximity to each other. His world could never operate like that; they would all kill each other within the first week.

The Deer was also amazed at the sheer *number* of humans. They all seemed to look alike, but there were still so many of them, unlike demons. There was only one Deer, one Rook, one Wolf, one Bear. There weren't that many of them anymore, and he couldn't remember the last new one. Perhaps it had been the Mockingbird, or maybe it had been the Fox, or maybe the Unicorn. Maybe it was even he himself.

Humans seemed to multiply daily, however. They didn't seem to understand the fact that there could only be so many of them existing at a time. Then again, the Deer wouldn't mind it if there were more demons. It meant that they each wouldn't be so well known by each other. A little bit of anonymity would be handy once in awhile.

The Deer snorted and shook his head. It was too late; he had tried to stay neutral, even going to meet with the Owl once; he couldn't change his mind now. He merely had to help the Cat and the Wolf as best he could by scouting out some of the human cities.

He jumped to another city and appeared in a park. It was green and trying too hard to mimic nature. He looked around himself curiously, trying to figure out why he had landed there. He often did that to try to quell the nausea that often followed teleportation.

Unfortunately, the Deer found out all too soon why he had arrived there.

He froze when he saw a dark-haired boy down the path. The boy didn't notice him and instead inspected flowers along the path. Right behind him, looking bored and slightly angry at the world, was the Rook.

Too late, the Deer's senses told him that the Rook was nearby. At the same time, the Rook slowly turned and noticed him. They locked eyes.

The Deer disappeared and flung himself to the ground when he came back to his own world. He immediately started coughing up blood, landing hard on all fours. He shed his human disguise and tried to get rid of the pain that way, but he had never performed a jump so quickly after another, and he couldn't shake the effects of it.

He eventually collapsed on his side, shivering and still weakly coughing up blood. The Deer had no idea if he would survive this, but he had to tell the others about this. He knew where the Rook was. He also knew, however, that if he tried to teleport to them he would die on the spot. His only chance was to wait and see if he could recover from this. The Deer lost consciousness.

The Rook stared long and hard at the spot where the Deer had vanished. They weren't safe anymore, unless the damned Deer had died from his hasty getaway. The Rook hoped so, but he couldn't be sure. It would be safer to move, anyway, just in case.

He was jarred out of his thoughts when Michael spoke up. "Rook, do you have a king?"

He hit the boy on the top of the head, reminding himself of the here and now. The Deer wouldn't be able to teleport again for awhile, especially after that last one, so even if he had survived and managed to tell someone about the Rook, they couldn't get to him just yet. "Of course I don't. Why would you ask a question like that?"

"I figured you wouldn't. You don't seem like the kind to follow orders," Michael said easily, rubbing his head. He looked back up at the Rook. "Is there any sort of ruler or ruling group, then?"

"Why are you so full of questions?" the Rook asked in reply.

"You told me not to ask a question to answer one," he muttered, looking away. The Rook rolled his eyes.

"First, look at me. Second, *you* can't. It doesn't mean I can't. Why do you ask?"

Michael glared up at him, eyes narrowed. "I've wondered for awhile, because you don't take orders."

The Rook laughed and slung an arm around his shoulders, forcing him to walk once more. They had stopped to look at flowers, of all things, but he wanted to start moving again. Any distance they could put between themselves and that spot would be good.

"You didn't answer my question," Michael added, tense from the touch. He had been like that ever since the episode with the Rabbit.

The Rook paused, wondering if he should tell him that he really didn't have to answer any question of Michael's. But then again, it wouldn't hurt to talk a little of the past. It was fun while it lasted, after all. "There's no real ruler of any sort. We acknowledge the strongest, though, and some of the weaker ones flock around them."

"Were you a leader or a follower?"

The Rook chuckled and dug his claws into Michael's shoulder. "I'm hurt that you had to ask that, Michael. Of *course* I am a leader." That was actually a lie. The Rook had never led anyone, and certainly not alone. Though it wasn't as if he had followed anyone. He just happened to ally himself with the Ram, and they often jockeyed for the dominant position.

"Who were some of the other leaders?" Michael asked, unable to hide the curiosity in his voice.

"The Owl has always been powerful, but she wasn't so aggressive about it like we were. The Phoenix and the Fox were both more antagonistic. Most of these groups were small, so it wasn't as if these were massive forces fighting with each other. Rarely did we fight seriously."

"...But you still did sometimes?"

"Naturally. How do you think I became a criminal?" the Rook joked, making sure his tone was kept light. Michael didn't respond and instead looked down at his feet. They left the park. The Rook wouldn't have minded leaving the city, too, but that could wait.

At least until after some more French fries. (He didn't want to admit it, but he was exceedingly fond of some human food.)

137

CHAPTER NINE

Blind As You Are Watching **Everything**

The Rabbit didn't argue with the Rook when he announced their move out of the blue. Michael had been expecting her to and was actually hoping for it; he didn't want to move. Staying in the same place for so long had made him attached to it. Not that he would tell the Rook that—although it was obvious enough—but he was fairly upset when they had to leave.

And leave without packing up anything! Michael had *belongings*, for the first time in years. He really didn't want to leave any of it, but the Rook would not budge on the issue.

Actually, it came down to scene that was so sad it was almost funny. Michael really, *really* didn't want to leave his large, very comfortable bed, especially to go live in the wilderness again. He had actually hidden under the covers and had grabbed onto his pillow (whether to use it as a weapon or a shield, he didn't know).

The Rook had responded to this by pulling the covers off and picking Michael and the pillow up, throwing them both over his shoulder. The Rabbit watched mutely, saying nothing about this development. "Hey—!" Michael shouted, almost daring to kick.

"Don't talk back to me. Shut up and hang on if you don't want to fall. That pillow won't do you much good if you do." It had been awhile since the Rook was so quietly serious. Michael tightened his grip on the pillow and scowled into it. The Rook carried them both over to the nearest window, shattered it with a kick, and nearly smacked Michael in the face when he brought out his wings. "Bun, run ahead to the second city to the west. Get Michael another place to live, since he's gotten picky and isn't satisfied with our mere company anymore."

The Rabbit nodded and darted off. Michael scowled harder into his pillow as the Rook shifted him so he wouldn't interfere with his flying. "…I hate you," he mumbled into the pillow.

"You don't mean it. If you ever did, I'd have to snap your neck," he replied curtly.

Michael peeked up at the Rook, brow furrowed. "What's wrong?" The Rook was physically abusive when it suited him, but usually the verbal abuse coincided with something serious.

The Rook stepped out the window. It took a couple heart stopping stories for his wings to halt their fall. He didn't respond even when they stabilized and flew off towards their new home.

The Rabbit flagged them down on the roof of another skyscraper in another city with another penthouse apartment. Michael wasn't arguing, but it seemed too surreal. The layout was entirely different, the view wasn't nearly as nice, and there were no bickering demons to offset his worry. The Rabbit just showed them where they were staying and disappeared into one of the bedrooms.

When Michael peeked in on her, he was both surprised and alarmed to find her curled up, sound asleep.

"I thought you said you didn't sleep," Michael whispered to the Rook, slightly accusatory.

"I didn't say that. Besides, I've slept before in front of you," the Rook replied sourly. He settled down on the couch, lying on his stomach, wings lying arbitrarily on the back of it. He set his chin on the arm of the couch and stared sullenly at Michael. "We have to sleep. Not as often as humans, that's all."

"How often?" Aside from the rather short nap the Rook had had earlier, he hadn't slept in over four years. Michael hadn't ever seen the Rabbit sleep, either, until that day.

"Roughly once in one of your years. But it's usually a full twenty-four hours." He glanced over towards the bedroom's open door. "I guess she's tired. It'll be awhile before she wakes up."

Michael was a little taken aback by the thought of a full day of sleeping. It also made him a bit scared to think that the Rook would have been asleep for that long if he hadn't called him. "But... You didn't sleep that long. You haven't slept that long *ever*."

The Rook returned his gaze to Michael. "So?"

"You should sleep! What if—what if you fall asleep while you're flying? What if you fell asleep on the way here?" Michael crossed his arms and tried his best to look angry, but he was more bothered than angered.

"I wouldn't. That would mean that I'd hurt you, so of course I wouldn't."

"But what if you *did*—"

"I'm not going to go to sleep," he said forcefully.

"Why not?" Michael demanded.

"You'll leave me again," the Rook replied in a perfect monotone. Michael stared at him, bewildered, and tried to come up with a decent response. What could he say to such a thing? The Rook had given him one of those annoyingly clear insights to how his mind worked again, and as usual, the boy didn't know how to take it or how serious he really was. The Rook blinked lazily and ended up closing his eyes before adding, "Plus, I am not stupid enough to sleep while the Rabbit is. You'd be unsupervised and that only ends up badly, doesn't it, Michael?"

"Yeah," he muttered, only because he didn't want to argue right then. Instead, Michael walked over and picked up the Rook's legs, moving them so he could sit down. The Rook huffed and moved his legs back onto Michael's lap. He tried to push them off, but they stayed firmly in place, so he figured he shouldn't try to instigate a fight. "Will you sleep tomorrow?"

"No."

"Why not?"

"I don't trust the Rabbit with you anymore."

"So you're not going to sleep until she leaves?" That didn't seem like it would be anytime soon. Plus, the last time the Rook had tried the insomnia approach, he had ended up nearly passing out. Michael didn't fancy suddenly and unwillingly giving up the Rook's protection like that again.

"Or until she dies, no."

"Don't kill her."

"Why not? She doesn't do much."

"She's the one who is helping us hide and getting us these nice places to live—"

"—And when she *does* do something, it's an attempt at you," the Rook concluded. Michael squeezed his eyes shut and tried not to think about that. "Why wouldn't you let me kill her for that?"

"I told you—sh-she's helping us."

"Aren't I enough for you anymore, Michael?" the Rook crooned, retracting his wings so he could roll over. "We did so well together on our own, before that whore came into the picture. Don't you miss those times?"

"Don't get into that..." he groaned, covering his face with his hands. The Rook sat up, pulling his legs off his lap. Michael gave a start at the movement and pressed himself into the corner of the couch, looking at the Rook only to make sure he wasn't moving in preparation for an attack. "It's not that, I promise it isn't," he bit out, smoothing the ruffled feathers before he'd get punished for them. "I... I'm..." Michael cast about for some clever lie to prevent the Rook from getting mad at him. The truth was that he *liked* living in the city again, with a bed and a pillow and food and the Rabbit as a sort of buffer between the Rook and himself.

He could hardly say that, though.

"You're too attached to the Rabbit," the Rook supplied with a tight smile. Michael stared at him with something akin to horror. He shook his head and opened his mouth to speak, but the Rook preemptively cut him off with, "That's not a problem, Michael."

"I'm not, I swear I'm not," he argued, weakly and shakily. It wasn't a lie nor was it the truth; he merely did not want to see the Rabbit killed. He felt indebted to her. He didn't particularly like her, not after what she had tried, but he couldn't stand to see her murdered in cold blood on his behalf. (Which was slightly odd; Michael originally had thought he would have been more used to such things.)

"Tell me she doesn't matter. Tell me I'm the only one that matters to you, Michael." The Rook once more had his attention, reaching forward and grabbing Michael's chin to force him to look at him. There was too much force in his voice for it to be another casually possessive demand.

"You're the only one who matters, Rook," Michael said. It was only half a lie.

The rest of the Rabbit's slumber was spent in the calm before the inevitable storm. She awoke with a wide yawn and a sleepy hug for Michael, before the Rook chased her off from even that. It was after that that she returned to keeping her distance from the both of them (but particularly Michael).

That didn't mean she wasn't going to talk, however.

"You haven't been *sleeping*?! If the Bear knew that, you'd have to answer to *her*, you know!" The Rabbit squealed and ran across the room, disappearing out of the Rook's claws as he dove for her.

"I don't care about that sluggish Bear, now quit your

screeching!" he snarled, kicking off the back of the couch to make another leap for her. She darted out of his grasp again.

"You're only going to fall asleep later on when it's at a very bad time, I hope you know!" she warned in a high voice, running to the other side of the room again.

"That's what I've been telling him," Michael remarked casually. He was seated on the couch, calmly drinking from a bottle of water as he watched the two race around. It was a miracle in and of itself that it hadn't been spilled yet—which was why he was drinking only water instead of something that stained. "He won't listen. But at this rate, he'll tire himself out, so…"

The Rook froze, perched on the windowsill, and contemplated this revelation. Then, very slowly, he eased back down onto the floor and folded his wings primly behind him. Michael still considered it a silent, slight win; the two weren't fighting anymore.

At least, they didn't fight for all of two minutes, until the Rabbit piped up, "I didn't know you took *orders*, Rook." All hell promptly broke loose after that. Michael jumped off the couch as if burned as the Rook finally caught up with her—much to her terror and pain—and they tumbled over the back of it.

When the blood started staining the couch, Michael decided to leave. He couldn't do anything for either of them, least of all the Rabbit. He didn't know why she was baiting him so blatantly or cruelly, unless it was her petty way of getting revenge. Though really, that didn't make sense, either, since she had to have known that the Rook would have been out for blood following such a comment.

Granted, there was no way she was masochistic enough to have planned on letting the Rook catch her, but still. The fact of the matter was that he *did*.

Eventually, when the Rook pinned the Rabbit against the far wall, Michael got the chance to properly escape. (He had been hiding under the table until that point.) He sprinted to the bedroom and slammed the door shut behind him. He also tried to move something in front of the door, but as the room was sparsely furnished and the lightest thing would have been a wardrobe, that didn't work out too well.

It barely took any time at all before the Rook tried to come in after him, but Michael sat in front of the door and silently prayed to himself that the lock would hold. Especially when it was apparent that the Rook's anger was still all too much on the surface. "Michael! Open this door—that's an *order*!"

There would be hell to pay later. A lot of it, and it would undoubtedly be very painful. But at least the Rook wouldn't have the thought that he had taken an order from Michael in his mind. That would make all the difference; when the Rook had calmed down and had eased into his "make Michael's life hell but keep him alive" mindset once more, Michael would much rather deal with him.

Because, if he was being honest with himself, he would not put it past the Rook to kill him to make a point.

Michael wrapped his arms around himself and ignored the yelling on the other side of the door. Occasionally he'd hear the Rabbit intercede, but that was usually followed by a scream or a very loud, very painful sounding thump. The Rook kept up a nearly constant stream of shouting and abusing the door all the while.

He didn't know what happened first, if he fell asleep or the Rook did. Hours had passed and remarkably, the door held up, or else the Rook had—for some reason—not wanted to break it down. Truthfully, he didn't even realize he'd fallen asleep until the white-haired woman in the blue dress walked up to him and told him, "Hello, Michael. I am the Owl, and I'm terribly sorry to trespass in your dream."

CHAPTER TEN

Where **Everything's Ours** For A Few Hours

Michael looked around him. He was sleeping? He hardly ever dreamt anymore, not after nearly constant nightmares following the end of his time on the island. But to have this person—the Owl?—just waltz into his dream and *announce* that it was a dream... It was more than unreal.

He was in a world devoid of life. The ground was a harsh, dry grey-brown that melded seamlessly into the steely sky at the horizon. The light was muted and soft, giving everything a hazy, overly dim look. Aside from rocks and cracks in the ground, the only outstanding feature of the grey world was a lone, dead, gnarled tree that hung despairingly over the Owl.

"This *is* a problem," she murmured with an uncertain smile. She looked around, mimicking Michael, until he was staring at her once more. "I apologize for trespassing, again. It was not my intention."

"You're the Owl?" Michael asked dumbly. The Rook had mentioned her when describing the ruling powers, and said she hadn't been aggressive, or something like that. She certainly didn't seem too hostile. He knew instinctively that she really wasn't human and only looked it, but the human bodies had to have *some* sort of relevance to the real ones, right? If so, then she was frail, delicate, and somewhat cheerful looking. Not something he was used to seeing in demons.

"Oh. Yes, I am. Has the Rook spoken of me?" she asked curiously, fixing her large eyes on him unblinkingly.

"He's... mentioned you."

"Once, when describing the power struggles our species often had prior to his crime and subsequent defection," she elaborated with a wide smile. Michael stared at her, mouth agape. *How* had she known that? Could she read minds? If so, he definitely didn't feel safe.

"How—?!"

"I have power over knowledge. This does not mean I read minds," her smile grew, "But it means that I know a lot, simply put. And right now, I know you are afraid of me and are wondering what is going on. I can't sufficiently answer either of those questions, I'm sorry."

Michael glanced at the dead tree hovering over her. "…Why not?" he asked quietly, addressing the longest branch.

"I didn't mean to come into *your* dream. I meant to invade the Rook's."

"Why his? Are you after him, too?" he asked cautiously. This was only a dream, so she couldn't hurt him physically—at least, he was pretty sure she couldn't. He didn't necessarily want to test that theory, but it meant he felt safe enough to make a couple of small demands.

"Not exactly. I just want him to try to fix what he's broken. Is that wrong to ask for?" she asked simply. She really seemed to want to know Michael's honest opinion on the matter.

So instead of giving the Owl a knee-jerk response, he looked down at his feet and thought about it. The Rook had committed a crime, and a pretty heinous one at that. He admitted it himself, too, so there really wasn't any question about his guilt.

But should he have to repent for it in some way? Michael had frankly never thought about that before. He couldn't see the Rook as the type to apologize for anything—let alone as the type to serve some sort of sentence for his crime. What *was* the demons' punishment for murder? Did they have the capital punishment? Obviously, the Rook was wanted for his crime and wanted pretty seriously, but Michael never thought about what would happen if he was captured, or what would happen afterward.

Michael frowned to himself. He couldn't believe what he

was thinking. "...Even if the Rook is responsible for this crime, he won't do anything. He won't apologize or repent or believe he did anything wrong at all. He won't feel guilty for it. And without that feeling, you can't truly punish him. ...If need be, he will go to Hell and that will be his punishment."

The Owl laughed at his answer. "I think I should have expected as much from you, Michael Sante. You might be good for the Rook, after all." He had no idea what that was supposed to mean, but he didn't like what it implied.

"You're not angry that I decided he shouldn't be held responsible?" he asked with no small amount of care. He wasn't quite sure if all demons were morally in the red or if it was just the Rook and Rabbit. So he really couldn't be sure if the Owl was humoring him or actually agreed to some degree with his decision.

It was also a decision based more on practicality than anything else, he realized. He simply knew that the Rook wouldn't do anything he didn't want to, and that undoubtedly included punishment.

"Why would I ever be angry with you, Michael?" the Owl asked, reminding Michael all too much of the Rook.

"What could you do to him in a dream?" he asked instead of answering her. He knew the Rook would not be coerced into anything, especially without the threat of physical harm.

"My dear human, do you really think I don't have a *little* bit of blackmail potential on that Rook? I *am* the Owl of wisdom, after all," she said with a tinkling laugh.

Not that Michael didn't believe her, but his belief that the Rook wouldn't respond to blackmail was stronger. The Rook wouldn't give in; he would much rather simply kill whoever was attempting to hold anything over his head. "...I didn't think of that."

"I also have reason on my side, don't forget. The Rook is in the wrong, and he knows it, so it's only a simple matter of persuading him to do the right thing." Apparently their kind *did* have morals.

"Good luck with that," Michael replied, still not completely convinced. The Rook was too strong of a character to do anything that would weaken that. To the boy, he was something like immortal. It wasn't that he thought he didn't die—for quite awhile after their meeting, Michael had hoped that the Rook would fall over, dead, and give him his life back—but more that he was untouchable. The Rook didn't bend. Maybe he would break eventually, but he would never bend.

"You might not have much faith in me, but assure me, I have a fair amount of confidence in the Rook." The Owl took a step towards him, and great, white wings burst out of her shoulders and curled around her. She stretched them once, then flapped them, and hovered over Michael with a benign smile. "I must go now. We still don't have much time, and I need to speak to the Rook. Thank you, Michael, for tiring him out so."

He found the fact that it was *he* who finally put the Rook to sleep more than ironic. Michael only watched mutely as the Owl flew off and disappeared from his dream.

When Michael awoke, it was dark out. He stood up and stretched, feeling sore after sleeping for so long in front of the door. He pressed his ear against it, and, after hearing no sounds, eased it open.

The Rook lay across the couch, looking as if his body had been dumped there. The Rabbit, sitting at the table, looked up. "He's been asleep for only a couple hours. He'll be out until tomorrow," she told him tonelessly, returning to a steaming mug.

Still unaccustomed to her distance, he seated himself opposite her. "You're glad for this?"

"It means a break of him, so yes," she said in that same flat voice. The Rabbit wouldn't look at him, eyes on the mug. "...It means a break of his criticism and narrow mind."

"Does he bother you that much?" Michael asked uncomfortably, fidgeting. He knew that most of her feelings towards the Rook had to be because of him. The Rabbit nodded, keeping her silence. When she didn't say anything else, Michael sighed and asked, "What do you know about the Owl?"

"Why?" At least she seemed a little more animated with the added curiosity. She risked a glance up at Michael through her bangs, probably wondering where he had heard of the Owl, or how much he knew.

"I met her," he said easily, hoping rather selfishly for some shock. He didn't get any, though she kept looking at him. "She appeared in my dream."

"...That means that she met the Bear..." the Rabbit murmured, eyes downcast once more. She sipped absently at her drink. There was something in her voice that stopped him from asking who the Bear was. Michael stayed silent; it was a long time until the Rabbit looked up at him again. She seemed surprised that he was there. "Was there anyone else with her?"

"No."

Almost immediately after his answer, she looked back down. Michael just about copied her movement, but caught himself just after he bowed his head. He slowly raised his head again, blue eyes locked on her brown hair. It matched the color of her drink, he noticed.

The Rabbit didn't speak again, nor did she answer his original question. The pair sat at the table silently for a long time instead, until she got up and wandered off like a sleepwalker to the kitchen, dropping her cup in the sink, and left out the door. Michael watched her go and didn't comment, not even to himself. He wouldn't have known what to say anyway.

Michael was alone, again, with nothing but a sleeping Rook as company. He could not stop thinking about the Owl, however, and her circular logic around things. She had been meaning to go into the Rook's dreams, but somehow wound up in Michael's instead. He wasn't sure why that had happened, unless it was something to do with the fact that he spent much too much time with the Rook.

Did that mean that the Owl was in the Rook's dream right then? Michael looked over towards the Rook. He didn't move (or breathe) or show any sign of the dreams he was having. Michael stalked over toward the couch, tiptoeing out of habit, until he was leaning over the back of the couch. The Rook didn't react to that, either.

"...What are you going to do," Michael murmured.

The Owl stated her goal was to try to get the Rook to atone for his crimes—somehow. Or at least fix what he had done. What would that entail for the Rook? For Michael? Would the Rook do anything at all for the Owl, or would he fight against her? Would he win? The Owl seemed pretty confident about it... There was too much he couldn't even begin to guess about. The only chance he had for more information was what the Rook would share with him, and that could only come when he awoke.

"What are you going to do, Rook," he repeated to himself, draping his arm along the back of the couch and laying his head on it. The Rook mumbled something in his sleep, frowned for the briefest moment, and rolled over onto his side. Michael stared down at him, then reached down, hesitantly, and moved the lock of hair that was falling into his face behind the Rook's ear.

Whatever it was he ended up doing, no doubt it would be

something that would cause even more chaos in their lives.

The Rook didn't wake up until the day afterward, like the Rabbit had predicted. Michael was astounded at how quiet it was without him awake, and how calm things were. It was also—dare he say it—incredibly *boring*.

Without running for their lives, watching the Rook and Rabbit run and fight, or even without the steady stream of physical abuse, Michael really didn't know what to do with himself. It was like the scene in the meadow all over again; without the constant that was the Rook hanging over him, Michael felt unbearably alone.

The Rabbit, on her return, gave him a grin that looked as if it pained her to create when she saw him half lying over the back of the couch. She hung up her fur jacket on the back of a chair. "...I don't know who is worse, out of the two of you," she remarked innocently, dropping the smile.

"What do you mean?" He raised his head to look at her, furrowing his brow.

"Most others just see the Rook hovering over you constantly and fretting over you and just... taking care of you. But only I get to see this side of your relationship, and it makes me wonder." She turned her back to him and pretended not to care, only tossing her words out casually.

Michael noticed, however, and glared. "What is *that* supposed to mean?" He might not think she was so harmless anymore, especially with the Rook still asleep, but he knew that he wasn't afraid of her. He really didn't know why she was baiting the Rook and him so much lately, but he knew she had better stop before she said something really terrible.

And if she just said what he thought she said, then she

might be toeing that line.

"I'm just curious as to when you started your attachment, that's all. I would have imagined that you weren't so…" the Rabbit trailed off, turning back to him with a bright, obviously fake smile. It soon faded before Michael's glower, however. She pouted, and pointed out, "Look at how you're acting. In my defense, anyone sane—even a human—would see how you are."

"And how *am* I?" he asked warningly, trying to copy the Rook's threatening tone. It didn't work out so well, but at least the Rabbit had the sense to look away and pretend like he had won. "Well?" he pushed.

"Nevermind," she replied lightly. When faced with his glare, however, she eventually gave in and explained more, if only a bit. "…It's just that I would not have expected you to have any sort of fondness or anything like that for the Rook—"

"I do not have any such thing. I am not fond of him! I—I hate him—" Michael knew it was a lie, at least that last part. It was true that he didn't like the Rook, but he didn't hate him. He just relied on him for protection and apparently, entertainment as well. Still, the Rabbit didn't have to know any of that. "He is constantly hurting me, so why would I like him?"

"Humans are surprisingly emotional creatures," the Rabbit replied ambiguously, sashaying out of the room. Michael snorted at her retreat.

"Well, what do you know," he muttered darkly.

"What are you talking about…?" the Rook muttered. Michael must have jumped a foot in the air, head snapping down to look at him. The black-haired man glared up at him rather sleepily with one eye, his arm over his other.

"N-Nothing," Michael stammered out, pressing a hand to his chest to make sure he hadn't had a heart attack from the shock. The Rook sat up with a yawn.

He then grabbed Michael around the shoulders and pulled him over the couch. It was then, too late, that the boy remembered how he'd been behaving prior to the Rook's daylong nap. He flailed wildly, trying to wiggle out of his grasp, but the Rook held him still and pulled absently at his hair. "First off, you're lying to me—I know you are. You are not *allowed* to lie to me, Michael."

"I-I wasn't—"

"Furthermore," the Rook continued as if Michael hadn't spoken, "What were you doing before, hmm? Why didn't you come out when I asked so nicely?"

"I—"

"Michael, it *hurt* me when you ran away from me like that. Why did you do that? Do you *want* to leave me? To hurt me? Why are you trying to do to me, Michael?" It was just like the Rook hadn't slept, like Michael hadn't almost argued with the Rabbit, like nothing at all had ever changed. They were back to normal again.

Even if normal had a tight and sharp hold on the nape of his neck and was pulling on his hair.

"I didn't mean to, I promise," Michael managed to get in, gritting his teeth in an effort to stop himself from gasping in pain. Whether or not he was attached to the Rook in any manner was irrelevant when it came down to the raw materials of their relationship: a good dose of physical pain, a dash of anguish, a pinch of emotional control and pressure, and, you know what, more pain. It didn't matter what sort of pain it was, not anymore—the Rook dealt in all kinds.

"Do you mean that, Michael?" The Rook let go of his neck in favor of tilting his chin back, forcing him to look him in the eye. He tilted his head to the side, frowning thoughtfully. "Did you really not mean to hurt me?"

"Yes." Did he really expect him to answer with anything else? Michael was not suicidal.

The Rook broke out into a wide, sharp-toothed grin. "Good, Michael. If that's the case then I'll forgive you." He yawned again and pulled Michael into a one-armed thing that might've been a hug, or perhaps a halfhearted attempt at crushing him. Michael wasn't completely sure, but if the Rook really had just forgiven him, then maybe he should try verbally giving in more often...

"...I can't breathe," he mumbled into the Rook's shoulder. He earned a wicked little chuckle, but at least his grip slackened a bit. Michael managed to turn his head and suck in a grateful lungful of air, releasing it in a relieved sigh.

"Oh, Michael. You're too amusing." Michael scowled and kept silent. Oh yes, the Rook dealt in abuse of all kinds.

CHAPTER ELEVEN

Well She's Not **Bleeding** On The Ballroom Floor Just
For The Attention

On the day the Rabbit died, everything changed.

They had been staying in their fourth city and had been on the run from the Wolf and Cat for nearly six months. The Rook never had brought up the Owl. Michael had wanted to ask, and nearly did on several occasions, but somehow never got the courage up. If the Rook hadn't encountered the Owl for some reason, then it would only be opening up a can of worms to ask about her.

But if he had... Well, Michael didn't know *why* the Rook wasn't talking about it, then. The Rook wasn't a quiet demon and often spoke his mind, even (or especially) when things were bothering him.

During that time, even without the potential problem the Owl posed, life went on. And, as always, it went on dangerously.

They never did see the Wolf and Cat again, though it didn't mean that they had a smooth time of avoiding them. The Rook had announced after their third move that he had seen the Deer and that meant that whoever was chasing them had a lot more power on his (or her, Michael couldn't help but believe, thinking of the Owl) side than what they had believed originally.

They did, however, run into others.

Michael saw the Deer on the second run-in with him. He practically appeared on top of him, after all. The Rook had immediately pounced on him and started tearing at him with claws and even teeth, and the Rabbit had managed to drag Michael out of the fray and a safe distance away before he was caught in any of the crossfire.

The Deer got away, however, by shedding his human disguise and goring the Rook through the shoulder with an antler. The Rook eventually healed, though he had a scar from it. The emotional toll from the incident was much higher. It showed that they had more concrete enemies than they had thought, for starters.

It also showed how fragile their lives were.

The Rook hadn't complained about his wound when the Deer vanished. Instead, he had complained about the fact that the Rabbit was nervously playing with Michael's hair. She scowled at them both, looked pointedly at the blood flowing freely from his shoulder, and pushed Michael back towards him.

Only a month after that, when the Rook was finally beginning to heal and didn't wince every time he used his arm, that they met the Snake.

This meeting was much, much more disconcerting. It was disconcerting partly because neither the Rook nor the Rabbit had sensed him coming. Either the Snake had some sort of stealth secrets that neither of them knew about, or they were too used to each other and couldn't sense other demons anymore. Michael didn't know which thought scared him more.

What *really* disturbed him, however, was the fact that *he* had to save the Rook.

Michael and the Rook had been shopping in a city market. Or rather, Michael was looking for food while the Rook kept a tight grip on his arm and whined about the crowds and lack of fries. The Rabbit was supposed to be with them, but she had long since wandered off with a male stranger.

Michael had felt a tug on his arm; the Rook had let go of him. He wasn't surprised, really, since he often ran off to look at different human foods and proclaim very loudly how they didn't look appetizing (or, once, upon trying an apple, exclaimed that the taste could never compare with Tuesday). Michael started putting distance between them, just in case of another scene.

He bought a head of lettuce and a dozen carrots before he noticed that the Rook hadn't returned. It wasn't as if his errands took all that long, but usually, the Rook reappeared at his side and commented on everything he bought. Michael looked around for his escort, slightly worried.

What he found, after some searching, would have been laughably bizarre in any other circumstances. The Rook was walking away from him, for starters, which rarely happened on its own. He was being led by a blond man who was walking backwards in front of him, taking great pains to maintain eye contact. Though he had no idea what was going on, he knew that it wasn't good.

Michael started forward—only to be caught around the waist by the Rabbit. "Let me—"

"Don't get near him," she said in a low voice, nearly a growl. She wasn't looking at either the Rook or the man with the light hair and instead stared at Michael's feet. "That's the Snake."

"What's he doing?" He was more curious as to why a fight hadn't broken out yet.

"The Snake can control you, well, to some degree anyway, with eye contact. Sort of like hypnosis. So if he spots you, then you'll either be under his control if he wants to bring you along, or completely paralyzed if he just looks at you." That was a very good reason not to go charging in there, Michael agreed. It also explained the Rook's docile behavior.

"Then what are we going to do? We can't just let him get away!" he hissed, trying to get out of her grasp. The Rabbit finally let go of him, but kept a hold on his shoulder to prevent him from running off.

"*You* are not going to do anything. The Rook is very aware of what's going on right now, and he'll have my throat if I let you get anywhere near that Snake," she snapped, pulling him back and putting herself between Michael and the Snake. He

161

opened his mouth to retort, but she placed a finger to his lips and gave him a small smile. "Don't worry, Michael. I'll get your Rook back for you. After all, the Snake can't catch what he can't see."

She disappeared as she ran off. Michael crossed his arms and kept tailing the Rook and Snake from a distance, trying to remain inconspicuous and unseen. It took a couple minutes for the Rabbit to do anything, but eventually, the Snake halted. It looked as if he very much wanted to look around, but he still kept his eyes locked on the Rook.

The Rabbit appeared behind him and tried to place her hands over his eyes. The Snake hissed and ducked out from under her, elbowing her in the stomach. He narrowed his eyes and finally tore his gaze away from the Rook. Michael started forward, but the Rabbit sent him a look just before the Snake rounded on her.

The Rook stood there, looking dazed. He didn't move. Michael inched closer. The Rabbit had closed her eyes and was darting back and forth in front of the Snake, obviously trying to lose him by hearing alone. She managed to circle around him and put her arm around his head, once again trying to cover his eyes. He reared his head back and bit her arm. The Rabbit screamed and dug her claws into the side of his head, but he would not let go.

Michael really, really hoped he wasn't a poisonous Snake. He finally made it over to the Rook, however, and tried to move him. It seemed as if he was rooted to the spot. He noticed people were starting to give them a wide berth, but at least no one was paying much attention to the brawl in the marketplace. One thing to be thankful for in the horrid situation.

Finally, the Rabbit managed to detach her arm from the Snake's mouth, though she lost a good chunk of skin for it. She held her arm and tried to wipe as much of the blood away as she could, before looking up and glaring at him. Too late, she realized her mistake.

Michael couldn't help but roll his eyes as the Rabbit froze and stared at the Snake, who calmly walked towards her with his unblinking gaze focused on her now. The Rook was still useless, too, so unless he wanted both of them to die or be carted off or otherwise leave him, he had to do something.

He looked around, making sure to avoid the Snake, and tried to find something he could use. If only he had claws like the Rook or Rabbit... Instead, his eyes alighted upon a pair of scissors hanging from a nail on one of the stalls. He dashed over and grabbed them before the woman managing the stall turned around and mentally made a note to return them if possible.

"You're terrible, Rabbit," the Snake told her, speaking for the first time. His low voice caught Michael off guard; he had been expecting something more like a hiss. He was now directly in front of the Rabbit and reached out a hand to tilt her chin back, as if studying her. "I heard from the Deer that you were spotted with the Rook... But I didn't think that you would fall so far as to join him. ...I suppose the rumors are true. You really are a whore."

It was the furthest thing from the truth, but if the Snake wanted to try to insult her, so be it. It bought Michael time. He managed to circle around the Snake, hoping to God that he hadn't been noticed yet. He gripped the scissors like a knife. A knife probably would have been better, actually, but he didn't have time to go searching.

He managed to get around behind the Snake without being noticed. Michael was holding the scissors so tightly in his hands that he nearly cut himself on them, but he didn't even notice. Instead, he crept up behind the Snake and held the scissors up over his head like he supposed would be the best way to stab with.

Michael paused when he saw the Rook move. It was barely a twitch of his arm, but he noticed it—and so did the Snake. The Snake immediately turned to look at the Rook, glaring slightly. Michael was unfortunately too close to the Rook still to escape detection, and the Snake turned to him in surprise. Michael immediately shut his eyes and ran forward.

He felt the scissors hit something and a loud hiss. He opened his eyes to find the Snake's arm shielding his face from the scissors; the blades were buried in his wrist surprisingly far. Michael swallowed thickly and wrenched them out, this time aiming for his neck. The Snake lowered his arm, though, just as the boy stabbed downward.

Michael was frozen, the tip of the scissors pressing lightly against the Snake's neck. The blond man surveyed him with irritation. "...You must be the Rook's pet I've heard so much about," he stated at last.

Michael really didn't like that title, but he couldn't argue. He didn't want to, either, since arguing with demons never got him very far in life.

Thankfully, since the Snake had turned his attention to Michael instead of the Rook, his paralysis wore off before anything drastic happened. Well, actually, *something* drastic happened—the Rook nearly killed the Snake in the middle of the marketplace.

Once it wore off the Rabbit as well, she hastily intervened and made them settle their dispute in a less crowded place. And, as before, she went around and subtly pick pocketed all of the humans courageous enough to try to record the fight on their cameras or phones. The Rook carried the Snake off (after the Rabbit blindfolded him) and Michael didn't see him until that evening. He came back with bloody hands and an angry scowl, and that was how they packed up and left for their fourth city.

It disturbed Michael to see the Rook literally lead along like that, and how easy it must be for other demons to kill one another without even fighting. For the first time in a very long time, he had nightmares. And for the first time in an even longer time, the Rook wasn't the villain in them. Instead, he was the victim—being maimed and killed by a plethora of other monsters that Michael's tormented mind invented for him.

Most of it was forgotten when he awoke, aside from a feeling of certain impending doom. Michael stuck close to the Rook, greatly confused by his anxiousness and how easily startled he was after the Snake's death. He caught the Rabbit looking at him whenever he jumped, but it seemed as if the Rook didn't notice in the least.

The day dawned spectacularly sunny and cloudless. Michael woke up feeling well rested for the first time in days. The Rabbit was already gone, or still out from the night before— he didn't know and he didn't particularly *want* to know. She may have helped in certain situations and may even be somewhat apologetic sometimes, but it didn't mean Michael really cared about her anymore. She'd had her chance.

At what, he didn't know. Nor did he know if the Rook had ever had that chance, or if he had, what had happened to it. He just knew that he preferred the Rook to the Rabbit.

The Rook was drinking his new favorite drink, coffee, and blatantly didn't offer Michael any. It wasn't as if he minded; he didn't like the bitter taste when he had tried it, and he knew the Rook didn't like to share. "Morning," he grunted instead, sitting down at the table.

The Rook smiled into his mug. "Look at how domestic this has become," he remarked unexpectedly.

"Huh?"

"Five years ago, I never would have expected this to be the result of finding you. It's terribly domestic, isn't it?" he elaborated after a lengthy sip of his coffee. Michael looked at him sideways. He was used to seeing the Rook go through his phases of human food and drink, but seeing him standing at the sink, staring at the window, placidly sipping his morning coffee. It really *was* domestic. Something like a normal household would do in the mornings.

Ignoring that and its implications (which Michael was sure would distress him if he thought about it at all), he asked, "Does that mean you searched me out specifically?"

"Of course," the Rook replied easily. Michael sighed. Years ago, that would have made him madder than anything else, the thought that the Rook had chosen him out of billions on Earth to pursue and torment. Now, however, he was a little too apathetic and used to the Rook to care greatly. It bothered him only slightly, and only in a very passive sort of way.

"Why did you choose me, then?" he asked dully, not because he particularly wanted to know, but because it *had* to be asked. Michael might regret it later, especially that night when he had time to think about it more in depth. Still, the Rook had to give him at least a little information about that subject. He owed that much to him.

"Because I *wanted* to," the Rook said primly, and that was the end of that. He obviously didn't think he owed Michael anything, especially not information. Or maybe he didn't tell him because of that. It was too early in the morning to try to figure out the Rook, Michael decided, and went to get himself some breakfast.

It was hardly noon when the Rook dragged Michael out. He wanted to explore the new city, just in case they had to know the landscape. Since that was becoming more and more of an issue, Michael didn't put up much of a fight. Plus, he found that it was easier to deal with the Rook in a public setting, since he was less likely to do anything too terrible.

"Why is it that humans have such a fascination with tall buildings?" the Rook asked conversationally, leaning back to look up at the skyscrapers. Michael shrugged; he didn't know. "I'll tell you why—they're trying to copy the birds and get to the sky."

"Humans *can* fly, you know. We have planes," Michael pointed out.

"They aren't courageous enough to fly without them," the Rook snapped with a grin, ruffling Michael's dark hair none too kindly.

"We really can't fly without them—"

"Exactly. So you're all still trying to reach the sky with those buildings of yours. Just listen to the name you gave them—*sky*scrapers." Michael decided to give up then and there. It wasn't as if the Rook was wrong, but it was more the fact that he was ignoring logic to get to his point. He couldn't argue with that.

"Where all are we going today?" he asked instead. The Rook shrugged. "Is there anywhere you *want* to go, then?"

"I don't know. Perhaps. Anywhere *you* want to go?" he shot back. It sounded more like a challenge than a question, at least to Michael's trained ears.

"Anywhere's fine," he replied noncommittally, shoving his hands in his pockets. The Rook chuckled and didn't respond.

The pair wandered the city aimlessly. Michael spent most of his time avoiding gazes and staring at the sidewalk. The Rook

167

spent the majority of his time staring up at the tall buildings, grinning at the mirrored surfaces and the sun's reflections on them.

"I want to go see this store," the Rook announced suddenly, making Michael jump. He didn't take any notice, and was instead dragging the boy into the nearest shop.

"Why?" Michael asked.

"Because it has stuffed animals," the Rook replied. It took a few moments for Michael to compute the phrase 'stuffed animals' with actual stuffed *animals*. He shuddered when they went in the door and passed a snarling bear.

"…Why does this fascinate you so much?" He would have thought that the Rook would avoid dead animals on principle. Well, it was true that he rather liked death, but Michael never would have guessed that that applied to things he didn't personally kill.

"I never knew humans did this!" the Rook chirped, laughing at a stuffed raven that was glowering at them from a high corner. Michael shuddered again; that might as well have been his cousin and he was laughing at its corpse. Literally laughing at a dead body. *That* was nice.

"I'm going to wait outside. Is that okay?"

"Why?" The Rook turned to him for the first time since entering the store. He looked vaguely, almost concerned, though probably more for the fact that Michael was leaving him than for the fact that Michael was uncomfortable.

"I don't like it in here. Can I please wait outside?"

The black-haired man sighed. "Fine."

Michael scurried gratefully outside. It was almost worse, however, than the inside of the shop. The crowds had really started to gather during the rush hour, and Michael found himself fighting to not get pushed back inside. More people than he could count ran into him, and he had to press himself up against the glass in order to avoid even more.

Just when he was thinking he had better go back inside, if only to get out of the way, a girl chatting excitedly on a cell phone accidentally ran into him. She squeaked in either fright or outrage, noticing Michael only after she bounced off him into another person. Unfortunately, the collision made Michael lose his balance and he fell onto another unfortunate stranger. Between the two of them, they caused quite the scene, especially after a woman fell over completely and tripped another two people.

It took a couple moments for people to stop making the dog pile worse, but eventually it did. Michael, having been hooked around the ankle by a flailing arm, got back up onto his hands and knees. A hand reached down to help him up, and he took it without a second thought.

The man who helped him up didn't even notice him as he turned to help the girl and her cell phone up. Michael could not help but stare, stunned, at the reddish brown hair, although now graying at the temples, and the soft voice saying, "Here, love," as he helped the girl up.

Michael opened his mouth to speak and nearly said his name aloud—before he caught himself. The businessman just in front of him must have noticed the boy staring at him, however, because he turned expectantly towards him. Michael flushed and ducked his head, immediately trying to head back into the crowd to disappear.

The man stopped Michael with a hand on the shoulder. The younger of the two looked guiltily down, wishing he could vanish like the Deer or run fast like the Rabbit. "My God..." the man murmured, staring at Michael with the look one would give a ghost. Or a murderer.

"I-I have to—"

"*Michael*? Is that you?" Silvermin asked in disbelief. Michael shut his mouth tightly and tried to escape again. This time, however, the man merely pulled him forward and wrapped his arms around him. Michael tensed instinctively but didn't try to pull away, too used to the Rook's embraces.

"...Hi, Mr. Silvermin," Michael mumbled into his shoulder. It wasn't like he could deny it. He was caught.

"Dear Lord, boy, I thought... Where have you *been*? It's been years!" Silvermin held him out at arm's length, looking him up and down appraisingly. Michael looked down, not meeting his gaze. "Well... I must admit, it was smart of you to dye your hair. I'd recognize those eyes of yours anywhere, though, so there was no sense trying to pretend like you hadn't seen me." He was trying to sound stern, or maybe he really was being stern—but Michael was still too used to the Rook. Silvermin couldn't intimidate him to save his life.

Speaking of saving Silvermin's life, Michael glanced towards the store. If the Rook saw him, he would undoubtedly recognize him, and that would be the end of the businessman. He had to get rid of Silvermin quick if he didn't want another death on his conscience. "I, um, I wasn't sure it was you," he lied in a mumble, unsure of what else to say. Human company made him nervous, and it was *Silvermin*, of all the people in the world, to recognize him.

"You look thin. Hell, you *are* thin. Have you been living on the streets?" Silvermin asked briskly, putting his arm tightly around Michael and steering him down the sidewalk. Michael wasn't complaining, since it would put them out of the Rook's immediate range of sight, but it made him even more nervous to be leaving his escort.

"Yes." Another lie. Still, it wasn't as if Michael could come

170

out and tell Silvermin everything.

"You're living on your own, then?" Silvermin asked, mostly to himself, glancing down at his watch. "Michael, you're coming with me."

"Wh-What?" Michael's head snapped up in alarm, looking at the man for the first time since the initial shock wore off. Silvermin looked almost exactly the same since the island, save a bit more grey in the hair and wrinkles around his eyes. Even that was not from age, though; the island had done that.

"I'm going to feed you a proper meal, since I know you haven't had one in too long." Too late, Silvermin made a face. Both of them knew that that was probably the wrong thing to say. Michael's stomach churned just from the memories. Silvermin backpedaled awkwardly, "Er... That is... I didn't mean that, Michael. You know I didn't."

"I know," he replied quietly. "But... I have to be going."

"Why?" Silvermin asked curtly, looking down at him. Michael averted his eyes. "Can you tell me honestly that you have a prior engagement, or are you just running away again?"

Technically, neither was true. Michael was only trying to run from him in order to save him and make sure the Rook didn't find out. Still, he wasn't a very good liar, and it seemed like Silvermin knew that. He might have a whole lot of misconceptions about Michael and his state of living for the past few years, but he seemed to be able to sense the lie.

"That's what I thought." Silvermin started walking again, leading Michael along by the shoulders. Lowering his voice, he added, "Michael, don't worry. I am not going to get you into any trouble."

That thought hadn't even crossed his mind. "...Why are you doing this, then?"

"Is it so terrible that I feel a little responsible? I spent a year in and out of the courts, defending you, you know. Neither of us were convicted of anything concrete. The only crime you have on your record is running away," Silvermin told him. Michael frowned. That was hardly the truth.

"I still have to go."

"After you eat a proper meal. We need to talk, Michael." That gave him a very cold feeling down his spine. Especially since the Rook would eventually notice his absence and tear apart the town trying to find him. Michael squared his shoulders and tried to swallow, bracing himself for the inevitable.

As it turned out, Silvermin really *had* felt responsible for all of those years. Not just for Tuesday's death, either—for everything that had happened. The only thing he had been able to fix, however, was keeping himself and Michael out of prison and worry incessantly about what had happened to the other survivor.

Michael felt sorry for him, he really did. He must have had a hard time, going through the process of defending them both for a crime they both knew was wrong. He had known since they met each other that Silvermin was the sort of man to try to take responsibility for as much as he could, and even if he couldn't quite do it in the end, he still *tried*.

"What have you been doing since then?" Michael couldn't help but ask at some point during the meal. Silvermin had taken him to a fairly fancy restaurant and ordered for them both. Michael wasn't picky and practically inhaled whatever it had been that was on his plate.

"I'm in business again. I've regained nearly all of my fortune from before that blasted boat ride, and my company is starting to recover its value as well." Michael didn't understand most of it, but he took it as good news all the same. At least one of them had gotten out of the situation somewhat well. "Have you been on your own for this long?" Silvermin gave him a hard stare.

He was still nowhere near as scary as the Rook, or even as the Rabbit when she got into her moods, but he still had a certain air of power and control. Michael wasn't afraid, but neither was he entirely comfortable. "Yes, I have," he replied clearly.

"Michael, that offer still stands."

"Hmm?"

"I told both you and Tuesday that you could live with me after the island. I would still be more than willing to—"

"*No!*" Michael hadn't been aware of how loudly he had spoken until other people turned and stared. He bit the inside of his lip and lowered his voice, avoiding Silvermin's concerned eyes. "I'm fine."

"If you're living on your own, you are not. A boy as young as you can't hold a job, nor can he take care of himself. You're either lying to me about living alone or you are trying to brush off my duty as a human being."

"It's not your duty to take care of me," Michael replied quietly, unable to help the bitterness in his voice.

"I've known you since your parents died. I tried to take care of you both on the island. I *know* what you—what *we* have both been through. No one alive could understand that, Michael, could understand the stress of that situation. I'm not going to kidnap you and make you return to civilization, but neither am I going to let you live this way for the rest of your life." Silvermin's voice got that hollow tone again, the tone that Michael hated. He cringed and shut his eyes tightly.

"I can't do that. I couldn't live near people again."

"You wouldn't have to. I own a cottage up north, secluded on the edge of a forest. There are no people for miles. If you want to be alone, you could be." Michael snorted at the thought; he would never be alone, even if he did take that offer. Silvermin furrowed his brows, frowning beneath his mustache. "I'm serious about this offer, Michael. I could never be any sort of parent to you, maybe not even more than a casual acquaintance. You wouldn't have to see me for more than a month or two out of the year if you'd like. But let me at least make this one apology, please, Michael."

"I have to go," Michael said shakily. He stood up, turned on his heel, and walked out. He was still shaking by the time he exited the restaurant and his meal was threatening to come up his throat.

Silvermin made him nervous, but what *really* struck a nerve was the fact that Michael really, really would have liked that offer. If it weren't for the Rook and Rabbit. If it weren't for any of the monsters tailing him (or the Rook), Michael might have had a chance at a semi-normal life. Well, as normal as he could be after what the island did.

Michael found the Rook still in the same shop, chatting excitedly to an obviously uneasy shopkeeper. Michael stood right next to him and didn't say a word about what had happened. The Rook didn't ask. Eventually, however, with Michael's arrival, he got bored of the dead animals and left with only conning the unfortunate shopkeeper out of a feathered dream catcher.

"Why did you get that?" Michael asked, trying to start a conversation. He wanted to get his meeting with Silvermin out of his head.

"Haven't you been having nightmares lately?" the Rook responded, gesturing to the feathers hanging from it. They were long and white, vaguely familiar. Michael was almost touched, at least until the Rook added, "I can't do much when you're waking up in such a mood, now can I?"

"No," he deadpanned with a sigh. "What sort of feathers are those?" He almost would have expected the Rook to get black feathers on principle.

"Owl."

Michael stared at the Rook. The Rook ignored the look and continued walking, twirling the dream catcher absently in the fading sunlight. Was that some sort of admittance as to seeing the Owl? There was no way it could be coincidence. Michael reluctantly tore his gaze away from the Rook, staring at the steps as they headed up to their apartment.

If he *had* seen the Owl, what did that mean? Nothing had changed in their immediate life or relationship, but then again, the Rook couldn't be that dense. He knew of the Owl, obviously, and the Owl herself said she was working on tracking the Rook down. So *why* get a dream catcher with owl feathers, and then announce that to Michael?

There was only one way to find out why the Rook was messing with his head now, and that was to ask. Michael took a breath and turned back to the black-haired man beside him. "Rook, have you—"

The door opened and the stench of blood hit them. The smell was so strong that it almost immediately caused Michael to gag and cut off his question. He covered his mouth and nose and turned way. The Rook scowled, tensed, and silently pushed the door all the way open.

Michael didn't need to go inside to see the blood splattered on the walls. The Rook dragged him in, however, so he could close the door. "Stay here," he murmured, stalking off towards the living room. Michael stayed as close to the door as humanly possible, shaking violently and trying not to throw up.

There was blood smeared on several of the walls, furniture was overturned or broken entirely, and the smell of the blood was getting to be too much.

There was a shout. Michael jumped and hit his elbow against the doorknob. Hissing in pain, he looked over to where the sound had come from. The Rook marched out of the hallway, wings flapping behind him in agitation. "That damn—that whore—that damned—" He slammed his hand against the wall, dragging his claws along it as he walked.

"What—What happened?" Michael asked thickly. The Rook didn't hear him and instead kept ranting, kicking, and scratching. Michael took a step forward, now really worried. "Rook, what happened?"

"That damned—I *can't believe him*!" the Rook screeched, shattering a window with a kick. Michael edged around him, glancing at the bedroom. The door was still slightly ajar. The Rook shouted hoarsely and worked at ripping more of the glass off the window frame.

Michael held his breath and made his way to the bedroom. He slowly opened the door. He wasn't sure what he had been expecting, but what he saw was probably not it.

Though he had never seen the Rabbit's demon form, he recognized it immediately, if only for the long ears and the cottony, bloodstained tail. She was obviously dead. Her skull had been splintered and crushed over one eye socket, and one ear had been ripped out and tied around her throat.

One leg had been pulled out of its socket and was lying on the other side of the room, broken and missing two of her claws. Her rib cage had been opened, and it looked as if she had been stabbed with one of her ribs. Her spine was completely snapped and her hind legs lay at an awkward angle.

Michael sunk to his knees, still clutching the doorknob. The Rabbit was dead. She was brutally murdered—by who? Why? Who had caught up with them?

Before he could even comprehend more than the fact that the Rabbit was *dead*, the Rook hauled him upright under the arms and dragged him out of the room. Michael sucked in a breath and tried to scream, but the Rook preempted him with a, "Damn him—come *on*, Michael, walk! We have to get out of here!"

"Wh-What—Who did this?!" Michael said in a high voice. He still couldn't move and was perfectly content to let the Rook half drag, half carry him out into the living room. The whole apartment looked like a war zone, though how much of it had been the Rabbit's murderer or the Rook's tantrum, he didn't know.

"Shut up, Michael." Michael shut up, though he continued trying not to sob. The Rabbit was *dead*, she was dead and whoever did it was still out there, probably looking for *them* next. The Rabbit was dead and the Rook was freaking out and Michael had no idea who it was this time out to kill them.

The Rook locked the door, slammed the bedroom door shut, and picked Michael up again. He jumped out the window, shedding feathers and cutting both of them on the broken glass, and he caught them on the updraft just outside.

"*This* is why we don't go to the city, Michael! Are you happy now?! I bet that whore sold us out, too—we have to leave, Michael. I hope you know that. This is worse than the Cat or the Wolf or the Snake or that stupid Deer. *Are you happy now*?!"

"How can you ask me that?!" Michael snarled, fingers digging into the Rook's shoulder.

"Because this is your fault!" the Rook screeched, "*You* are the one who wanted me not to kill that Rabbit, who said she could travel with us, who was too attached to that whore! It wasn't me, Michael!"

"N-No, it wasn't me—"

177

"It was just like Tuesday! *You* killed her, Michael! It was *your* fault—"

"Shut up shut up shut up!"

The Rook halted in his flight and dropped Michael. Michael screamed and managed to grab onto the Rook's foot, but he was still left dangling over the city, far above the ground and hanging on for his life.

"Let me up!" he wailed, swinging pitifully in the air. The Rook scowled at him and kicked his leg, trying to dislodge Michael. He clung desperately to his pants leg and refused to let go. "What are you doing?!"

"You do *not* tell me to shut up!" the Rook shouted hoarsely.

"I'm *sorry!*" Michael couldn't believe he had to apologize to save his life, but really, it wasn't the worst thing the Rook had ever done to him. Blaming him for the Rabbit's death was worse—even if he had a certain logic to the accusation. If they hadn't come to the city, or if he hadn't insisted on letting the Rabbit help them, she wouldn't have gotten caught up with them, and she wouldn't have died... "Please, Rook, let me back up!"

The Rook finally managed to kick Michael off, but before the boy could do more than suck in a breath for a scream, he dove down and plucked him out of the sky. Michael stayed silent and shivery, unable to form anything coherent anymore. First he found the Rabbit's mangled body, then the Rook had dropped him mid-flight. It was not shaping up to be a very good day.

"Did you learn your lesson, Michael?" the Rook asked, almost gently, almost comfortingly. Michael nodded miserably. He wasn't sure what lesson he was referring to or if he actually had learned it, but he was beyond doing anything but agreeing passively with the Rook. He was alone with him once more.

"Where... Where are we going now?" he asked in a small

178

voice. They couldn't live in the city anymore, not without the Rabbit supporting them. Nor did he think he could handle living in amongst humanity again. Even if it would be in a different city, far away, he couldn't do it. Not without the Rabbit.

"I'm not sure. We have to go *somewhere* though, and quickly. At least if we want to get away. Michael, you know I'll keep you safe, right?" The last remark was so offhand that Michael almost didn't catch it. He did, though, and it worried him. The Rook only acted protective if there was some sort of threat.

"...I know where we can go," Michael said quietly, closing his eyes.

That's how Michael ended up smiling placidly at Silvermin once more, sweetly telling him that he would love to go live in his summer home far away.

CHAPTER TWELVE

I Raised My Claws At The **Darkness** And Ripped
The **Night** Apart

"I really appreciate this," Michael said for the millionth time.

"It's the very least I can do. Please, make yourself at home," Silvermin replied, gesturing absentmindedly to the empty room. "I'm afraid there's not much here, but what is here you may use. I'll have it stocked with more food soon."

Michael was about to reply with the fact that he could very easily get his own food, but realized in time that that would lead to too many questions. He tried his best to smile instead. It was hard to. "Thank you."

"I'll be back within the month, and will probably spend the winter here. Otherwise, this will be yours during the summer months, if you'd like."

"I wouldn't mind your company," he lied. He had to be nice to his host, though, especially an unwitting host who had gotten two for the price of one. He didn't know how the Rook was going to follow him here, especially after that plane ride, but he knew that the demon would undoubtedly follow him.

He had made sure the Rook promised not to kill or harm Silvermin in exchange for going through with the plan of using his cabin in the middle of nowhere. It had taken some wheedling with the Rook, but it wasn't that hard to track down Silvermin again and say that he changed his mind. The businessman looked all too happy for it. Relieved, even.

"Are you *sure* you will be alright here by yourself?" Silvermin asked, yet again. He looked at Michael curiously, eyes half narrowed. The dark-haired boy again tried to smile, failed miserably, and just nodded.

"Yeah. I will be. I'm used to it." He could not let Silvermin know about the Rook. The Rook had promised to stay out of sight whenever Silvermin visited, and while he wasn't exactly sure how the winter would go, at least it was a start. Plus, at the *very* least, they had managed to put a couple hundred miles between themselves and that city with the murdered Rabbit.

"...That's... good," he replied haltingly. He didn't seem sure of what to say. For the briefest moment, it was like they were back on the island. Silvermin was well intentioned, yet again, but still so terribly awkward and going about helping in all the wrong ways. The road to hell was paved with good intentions.

Michael continued smiling blandly, though it pained him to even try to act happy so soon after the Rabbit's death. He may not have liked her that much—or maybe he had, really?—but her death left too big of an impact on him for Michael to be able to function normally again.

"...Well, I'll be seeing you at the week's end. I just need to take care of some business. Then I will be back and I'll help to get this place in better living conditions. ...Right." Silvermin stood around uneasily for another few moments, then stuck out his hand. Michael took it loosely. The handshake seemed too much like a contract he couldn't get out of later.

Silvermin left Michael alone. He didn't have anything to unpack, so instead he wandered around the house. It was homey, that was for sure, with its large fireplaces and large paintings and animal skin rugs and log-cabin-ness. There were three bedrooms, a study turned library, a rather big kitchen, and a grand living room with the largest fireplace of all and a great view of the forest outside.

That was all well and good, but instead, Michael went outside. Cupping his hands around his mouth, he called, "Rook!"

"Oh, I thought he would *never* leave. Is he honestly going to be here all through the winter as well?" Michael whirled around to see a black bird perched on a tree stump near the corner of the house.

"Rook?"

The bird tilted its head to the side. "Yes?" he asked, clicking his beak. Michael put a hand to his mouth to stop himself from laughing. It had been too long since he had seen the Rook as an actual rook, and the effect was a little comical. The bird cawed and flew at him, pecking his head sharply as he passed. "What's with that, hm?"

"Nothing," Michael lied with a real smile. "It's just nice to see you so relaxed."

"Relaxed?" the Rook asked in disbelief.

"You haven't been a bird since we first met. You always prefer something else, something larger, something you can fight with."

"I can fight with this just *fine*, thank you!" he huffed, fluffing up his feathers angrily. Michael stifled another laugh.

"You're very small, though."

"I am still large enough to make you bleed!" he snapped, pecking Michael's hand as he landed on his shoulder. He jabbed his beak into Michael's ear just to make sure he got the message. The boy most certainly did as he yelped and clapped his hand to his ear, narrowly avoiding cuffing the Rook as well. "Point proven."

"Yeah…"

The week passed all too quickly, and before they knew it, Silvermin was back. The Rook moodily hid himself, though at night when the businessman was asleep, he came out and talked to Michael. He didn't even mind it if the boy was asleep, too. It seemed as if he just wanted Michael's company—though really, that had been what this entire thing was about.

On the third day of Silvermin's reappearance, he introduced Michael to an associate of his. It was actually an accidental meeting, since Michael had walked in on them discussing something in low tones, wanting to know if he could go into the hot tub. (Actually, the Rook had wanted to go in, being fascinated with humans and their bathing rituals in general.)

"Oh," Silvermin said, cutting off their discussion rather abruptly. Michael stared, a little blindsided, at the new man. He had thick, curly, light hair and equally light, hazel eyes. The man only gave Michael a once over before returning his attention to Silvermin. "...Remington, this young man is a personal friend of mine. Michael, this is Remington, a business partner."

The man, Remington, smiled coolly and nodded towards Michael. "A pleasure."

"Um, likewise," he mumbled. He felt skittish meeting new people, especially when he knew for a fact that the Rook was waiting just outside. He decided to bow out without asking for permission. Instead, that night, the Rook dragged him out and threw him in the hot tub anyway.

"Why are you so sulky? Don't humans like hot water?" the Rook asked, sitting on the edge. He was dipping his feet in, not too keen on getting all the way in once he realized that his wings would get wet.

"...Mr. Silvermin has a business partner over. I guess I didn't think there would be anyone else here ever besides us," Michael sighed, leaning on the edge.

The Rook rolled his eyes. "You're paranoid. Don't worry about it. We're only in trouble if someone *important* manages to find us."

It was Michael's turn to roll his eyes. It seemed that after they came back out to the country, the Rook was too relaxed. It might have been that he was putting on a front, but even so, it was a little irritating when Michael was the only one worried about what could happen and who could potentially be after them.

"I'll protect you, Michael," the Rook added seriously.

"Don't say that." Whoever had killed the Rabbit had done it brutally, but with obvious skill. He didn't doubt the Rook's fighting ability—he was just worried what would happen. The Rook still seemed invincible, however, even with the wound on his shoulder and the Snake leading him so easily astray.

Michael, on the other hand, was not invincible.

No matter how selfish it was of him to think that (or maybe the Rook was just rubbing off on him a bit too much), he still thought about it. He had already been used several times to either bait the Rook or as a shield against him. One of these times, someone was going to go over the edge and Michael would be the one to suffer for it.

He already had a complex about mortality, so this really wasn't helping things. Michael exhaled softly, hoping the Rook wouldn't comment again. Changing to the subject, he mumbled, "What if Mr. Silvermin finds out about you?"

"Why do you even have to ask? The man would probably panic and do something stupid. Oh, and I would have to kill him for you, of course," the Rook hummed, kicking his feet and splashing Michael in the process.

"Keep it down. If someone hears us, then—"

"Then I'm out of here, and you have the awkward duty of explaining why you're in the hot water at one in the morning."

"…Yeah, that." The Rook grinned happily, so Michael added, "That'll only make Mr. Silvermin suspicious of me, or maybe even get me in trouble. If he starts keeping an eye on me, you can't hang around so often anymore."

This caused the man to pause and think. Michael smiled to himself, somewhat satisfied that he had won, even if for a moment. "…Well, if he came too much in between us, I would have to kill him."

"What of his business partner?"

"Him, too. And whoever else is in that house of yours." The answer came easier this time.

"They're both businessmen. Eventually... Someone would notice their absence. It would only get messier from then on out."

"Michael, I'd kill *millions* for you. Even better that they're humans trying to take you from me. Why don't you understand that? No one's going to come in between us."

Around mid-November, Silvermin moved in for the winter. With him came Remington and an astounding amount of chocolate. It meant that the Rook had very little actual time with Michael anymore, and most of that was spent when the boy slept, which only made the Rook more irritable.

The house was far from bustling or warm or even happy, but there was a certain amount of comfort in living with other human beings. It was almost like living with the Rabbit again, only with less sexual advances and demonic fighting and more awkward conversations and actual food.

Silvermin turned out to be a decent cook, which was great, since Michael and Remington were not. Whenever Michael was roped in for a meal with them, they spent it talking business in hushed tones. Silvermin tried to make polite conversation, often dragging the curly-haired man into it as well, but it turned uncomfortable too fast. Michael was fine with eating in silence; it just took a couple attempts for the men to realize that.

Michael stayed out of their way as best as he could, but since the winter weather was closing in, he could go outside to hide in the forest with the Rook less and less. It wasn't as if he minded the cold, but he got too many questions and concerns when he spent hours outside in zero degree weather.

The air in the house was tense because of this.

Silvermin and Michael shared a bond, and it was obvious that Remington was left out of that loop. Silvermin and Remington, though, were business partners and spent most of their time together, so Michael was excluded from that. And Michael and Remington... Well, they usually tried not to spend too much time together without the buffer that was Silvermin.

The Rook, due to his frustration with the situation, became riskier and riskier. More than once, Michael had entered his room to find the black-haired man reclining on his bed. Michael felt it was only a matter of time before the Rook was discovered and that was the end of his comfortable time in Silvermin's cabin, but the Rook scoffed at his worries.

"Would I be so stupid as to get myself caught?"

"...I just don't want to have to think about that possibility. Could you please not come out at random anymore?"

"I only do it in your room. Be thankful for that. Besides, it's *cold* outside, as you're so fond of telling me lately. I don't want to have to spend all of my time out there alone." It very nearly sounded like the Rook was whining. Or, rather, he was; Michael almost thought he was whining about losing his company.

"Rook, this was part of our deal," Michael sighed, holding his head in his hands.

"I don't like the deal anymore," came the sharp reply.

"Can't we just survive this winter? We will have the rest of the year to stay here by ourselves then, and we could leave before the next winter. All you have to do is survive a couple more months. That's no time at all in your time, isn't it?"

"Time doesn't pass at different rates for us, Michael," the Rook deadpanned. "We just live longer and have less to do in

187

that time."

While Michael puzzled what exactly that meant, the Rook stood up. He stretched his arms and wings languidly, walked over to the dresser, and started pushing it. Michael only stared as he pushed it over in front of the door. "What—"

"Tomorrow, I'm not sharing. You can yell at them through the door that you're sick or angry or depressed or something. But you're staying with me," he announced, leaning on the dresser.

"But—that's crazy! They'll wonder—they'll get suspicious—this is *not* a good plan."

"I always come up with good plans," he pouted, narrowing his eyes at Michael as a warning. "They won't question why a young boy wants to be alone for one day. In fact, they should thank me for it. I have seen how the red-haired one acts around you. It's like you're some sort of animal he has to take care of, but he's not quite sure how."

"That's not true," Michael muttered. The analogy was off, even if its meaning was more or less the truth. At least Silvermin was trying, though. Michael had to give him that. He was already leaps and bounds ahead of the Rook on the caregiver front.

"Really? I think it is. The red-haired one doesn't know how to treat you, and it sounds like that other human would rather slit his own throat than have to socialize with you for more than ten minutes at a time. Don't bother denying it. *I'm* the only one who treats you nicely anymore, Michael, and you know it."

The logic (and truth) behind his words made Michael grind his teeth. "…Yeah." He hated how the Rook was getting to know more about humans and their interactions. Especially when he chose to throw these facts in Michael's face.

So, while he received many sidelong glances and a couple stammered out questions the day after, Michael spent that one day in his room with the Rook. It was a little difficult, reminding him to keep his voice down and not to make too much noise, but it didn't seem like there was too much suspicion afterward.

Well, aside from when Remington came into his room that morning and asked, "Is there something wrong, Michael?"

It was probably the first time he had ever approached Michael on his own. It caught him off guard, and more than thankful that the Rook had already left for the day. He didn't know where he went, but since he hadn't been caught yet and it had been going on a little over a month, he figured it was a good enough hiding spot.

"No." He very nearly asked 'why', too. Michael fidgeted and played with his blanket's hem, avoiding looking Remington in the eye. "...Is Mr. Silvermin worried or something?"

"Frankly, yes. We are both aware that you're quiet, and even have some antisocial tendencies, but you've never locked yourself in your room all day before. Are you angry with one of us?" That seemed to be more like the point. If it was merely emotional self-preservation, Michael could relax. The Rook hanging around made him nervous enough without the added worry of the two businessmen.

"No I'm not. Sorry to have worried you." It was only a half-lie. He was more glad that they didn't seem too suspicious, and Silvermin himself had just dismissed Michael's day in easily. Remington looked as if he wanted to say something else, even going as far as to open his mouth, but instead sighed mutely. He stood up and left the room soon after that.

It was two days later that Michael received the same talk from Silvermin. Not *exactly* the same talk, sure, but it boiled down to the same meaning: they were not suspicious, they were slightly curious, and they wished he would not do it again.

"Are you tired of them yet?" the Rook asked conversationally. He didn't venture back into the house itself for two nights following the lock-in. Michael didn't know if it was because of some sort of newly formed sense of discretion or if it was because the Rook felt badly for making Michael do that. But no, that would imply that the Rook cared about Michael in more than a… whatever manner he did.

"Why?" he asked disinterestedly. He had the Rook's ram skull on his lap and was lazily tracing the curves and ridges on the dark horns.

"I'm getting tired of having to leave you. They're annoying, too. When can I kill them and when can we move on?" he complained. He was perched on the windowsill, one knee drawn up to his chest. "I should just kill them now. I'd be nice, Michael. I wouldn't even wake them up."

"Don't do that."

"Is that an order, Michael?" the Rook asked with a daring, sharp-toothed smile.

"Of course not. I just… It's comfortable here. Can't we at least wait out the winter?" Michael didn't look at the Rook and kept his eyes on the skull in front of him. Years ago, he would have sooner cut out his own tongue than spend this much time looking into those empty eye sockets. But now, it was almost preferable than the Rook's cold, coal eyes.

"Mm, maybe. Only if they behave themselves."

"You promised."

"I could break it. I think I get a freebie by now. We've known each other *how* long? I'm pretty sure I get a freebie, don't I, Michael?" the Rook baited.

"You used your freebie with the Rabbit."

"When?" Now he sounded almost cross. Michael continued running his fingers over the horns. This skull had been the Ram's once. Before the Rook had decided to rip off his skull and steal it and become a criminal even by demonic standards. Before he

190

had found Michael and made his life hell. "*When*, Michael?"

"I don't know. But you two were always fighting. I figure you used up your freebie with all of that," he said softly. Maybe he could actually win this argument. If that failed, then he could always pressure the Rook on his promise. And if *that* failed, well... They would need a new place to live. Or they could even live there, in that cabin, and pretend that two businessmen hadn't been murdered in cold blood in the vicinity.

"...So what if I did? I could just go and kill those two others and you couldn't stop me. Could you." It was another challenge. Michael petulantly closed his eyes and scratched at the horns.

"Rook, just—don't. Please don't."

"Okay Michael. Because you asked nicely," the Rook chirped.

There was a brief period of silence. Michael slowly relaxed and resumed studying the ram skull. This had once been another living being's *head*. "...Rook, why did you steal the Ram's skull?"

"Because we were fighting. I won," he declared, as if it weren't obvious.

"No, I meant... Why did you rip off his head? Were you that angry with him? Or was there some other reason behind it?"

"...I'd be lying if I said I didn't think it'd give me a strength boost. I think it might have, too, but not up to his level. Maybe I was just trying to steal his power."

"Maybe?" the boy prompted.

"*Maybe*. Maybe I just wanted the satisfaction of severing his spinal column from his skull. It hurt for months after I swapped, though. I might not have done it if I knew it'd hurt that much." It really occurred to Michael then that the Rook had to have taken off his *own* head—somehow—in order to take the

Ram's. Or maybe there was some sort of big monster ritual about it. Even so, the Rook didn't have his own head anymore.

"Did you really hate him that much?"

"Maybe I did."

"Why aren't you sure?" The Rook took killing casually, true, but he always seemed so sure of himself and his feelings. Now he seemed to be fielding the questions.

"I don't know. Maybe because I don't want to think about that damn Ram right now," he said simply, reclining against the windowsill with a rustle of feathers. "...Sometimes, I really did hate him."

"But only sometimes, right?"

"Only sometimes. I guess."

CHAPTER THIRTEEN

And When You See My Face I Hope It Gives You
Hell

Michael kicked his legs aimlessly under the table. With each knock against the bottom of the table, Silvermin and Remington both flinched. At the same time. He kept doing it, precisely for that reason, because he earned the same reaction each time. He sipped at his hot cocoa, watching the men cringe each time his foot made contact with the wood.

Neither of them said anything to stop him, though. Which is probably why he continued it.

It was already nearing the end of December, and they were all still alive. That was good. The Rook was still as annoyed as ever at having so little time with Michael, but he hadn't gone on a killing spree just yet. Michael considered it a personal victory. He had successfully saved two lives for another few weeks.

Still no one came and found them. The Rabbit's murderer was still out there, somewhere, probably trying to find them. But they hadn't yet. So that was another good thing.

Kick, kick, kick. Silvermin's head bowed down a little more each time. Michael wondered if he was even aware of it.

"—okay, you can *stop that* now," Remington finally snapped. His nails had dug into the wood surface of the table, and he flicked bits of it out from under them. Michael smiled blandly and stopped kicking the table. Maybe the Rook was rubbing off on him a bit too much.

Silvermin let out a very relieved sigh.

"Silvermin, I'm getting impatient." And just like that, he was tense again. Michael watched them curiously. They often discussed business at the table, things like stocks and bonds and trying to find competition and destroying other companies in vicious takeovers. Or so Michael assumed. He didn't understand business; a grade school education didn't help that. "We have the goods, don't we? I just want him to show up so I can get paid."

"Relax. You'll get your end of the deal soon enough."

"Will I? Sometimes I wonder." Remington seemed particularly annoyed today. Michael sipped at his cocoa again, slowly sliding down into his chair. "When I entered into this deal with you—"

"*Enough*, Rem. In due time, all in due time."

Michael sometimes wondered how the island had twisted Silvermin. It was obvious he had taken some of his attitude back into his business with him, but it sounded sometimes like some of his deals were somewhat shady.

He was fairly certain that he wasn't the only one with dirty little secrets, though.

At the start of the new year, the Rook took to sleeping with Michael inside. Michael was not thrilled with this. Not only was the Rook grabby at night, but he didn't *sleep*, which meant that Michael would be vulnerable and unconscious with a demon *staring* at him all night. There was also the matter of the uncommon—but still problematic—wake-up call Silvermin would sometimes give him.

The Rook hadn't been caught yet, but Michael was starting to sweat over it.

"Rook, get *off*," he growled sleepily, rolling over. The Rook had him pinned between the wall and himself, and had woken him up in the process.

"It's so warm in here though," he whined, trying to hold Michael still. The boy was still too drowsy to think, though, which meant he was starting to fight back physically. "It's too warm."

"Then why are you coming *closer*. I have body heat," he said waspishly. He used the wall beside him as a brace to try to push the Rook away from him.

"Just shut up and stop it, Michael." The Rook eventually managed to hold his arms and used his wings to drag Michael back over to him. He fell back asleep grumpily in the Rook's arms.

And woke up in them, too.

For a brief moment, he thought it was still late at night because of the shadow the Rook's wings cast. But eventually he saw the bright morning sunlight on the wall above him.

"You slept in late," the Rook remarked.

"You're still *here*?!" Michael screeched, practically teleporting out of bed and across the room. He pointed at the window. "Out, out! Before Mr. Silvermin or Mr. Remington comes in!"

"If you hadn't started squawking and making all that noise, they wouldn't have—" the Rook started.

"Michael, is everything okay in there?" Silvermin's voice was suddenly straining through his door. Michael whirled around back to the Rook, but he was already gone, a few black feathers haphazardly sticking out of his blankets. He hastily pilled the blankets up over the pillows to cover them up, just as Silvermin knocked and finally entered. The businessman surveyed the room warily. "I heard you shouting..."

"Um, yes. I just—I just fell out of bed. Sorry," Michael told him, somewhat breathlessly. The Rook had managed to dodge a bullet there, and just barely. They would have to be careful again.

Silvermin gave him an unreadable look. The dark-haired boy avoided his gaze and wrung the bottom hem of his shirt.

"I had a nightmare," Michael added in a sudden stroke of genius. Silvermin immediately softened.

"I'm so sorry, love. I... I'm sorry." With that, he left the room. Michael sunk back onto his bed with an immense sigh. He felt bad for deceiving Silvermin (yet again), but at least that was a perfectly logical explanation and one he could use repeatedly to boot. That would hopefully explain a lot of things and deflect doubt at the same time. It was also something that Silvermin couldn't fix, not really, and would have to leave alone.

"Smooth," the Rook whistled, reclining, once again, on Michael's bed behind him.

"Get out."

And so the days passed. Michael was slowly getting used to the living arrangements, and the two businessmen were adjusting to his presence. The Rook didn't like it, but there wasn't much they could do. The winter was half over. It would only be a little longer before Silvermin and Remington left.

"Mid-March, I'd assume," Silvermin commented. "Remington and I will leave then."

"Actually," the pale-haired man in question spoke up, "I think I'll be leaving before that." Silvermin and Michael stared at him, surprised, and Remington continued eating nonchalantly.

"Er—why?"

"I have some business to take care of down south." There was careful emphasis on the word 'business'. Once again, Michael had the feeling that their business together wasn't completely clean. "I probably won't return here. Actually, Silvermin, I may need your help with that venture. There are these two idiots who are just giving me trouble and I want to get rid of them."

"Is that so," Silvermin mumbled. He scratched his beard, glancing furtively at Michael. "...I'm not sure I feel comfortable leaving Michael alone like that." The boy ducked down at being dragged into the conversation. He wanted to tell them that he wouldn't be alone, if only for the comfort it would give Silvermin. He really didn't like constantly lying to him.

"I'll be fine."

"You see? The boy will be fine for a couple extra weeks. If it'll take that. I just need your help in securing the assets of those two. You can return afterward if you'd like." Remington smiled warmly.

"Are you sure you need my help?"

"I'm sure I could handle it without you, but I'd greatly appreciate it."

Michael had a feeling more was going on in this conversation than what he was getting at face value. It probably concerned a pretty hostile corporate takeover. Or maybe it was even darker than that; they could be with the mafia, or they could be killing their competition themselves, or a variety of things. Business today was rough.

"In that case, Michael, I suppose I'll be leaving towards the end of the month. Are you okay with this?"

"I'll be fine," he repeated. The Rook would be delighted with this news, no doubt. He, on the other hand, really was not. It would mean no more human company, no more good food, no more hours on end without the Rook's company.

"...In that case, who wants dessert?" Silvermin asked brightly. With that change of the subject, Remington and Michael fell silent again. He brought out what appeared to be some sort of chocolate dish, which made sense, considering Silvermin's obsession with it. Remington usually skipped out on dessert, but it looked as if he was going to stay for this one. Michael surveyed him over his bowl.

"Will you be coming back afterward? I'm just wondering if I'll have to enter in another plane ticket to the books. And I'm sure Michael here is wondering that as well," he commented, idly tapping his spoon against the table.

"I think I may, if only for a couple weeks," Silvermin

replied. He seemed much more interested in his chocolate than the conversation.

"Slow down. You'll get a heart attack eating so much so fast," Remington pointed out. He sounded irritated. Michael couldn't help but fight down a smile, however terrible it made him; the Rook would probably die laughing if he found out Silvermin had died of causes other than his claws.

"People don't get heart attacks from sweets. Only fatty foods."

"Aren't sweets supposed to be fatty?" Remington looked down at his dish with a new eye. Carefully, he took a bite, and spit it out not a moment later. "More of your chocolate. I *know* that's fatty. You will get a heart attack and die, Silvermin, and then you'll never see the end of our deal. Won't that be a shame."

"Yes," Silvermin said dryly, glaring at Remington. He seemed offended for the badmouthing of chocolate. Michael watched them both mutely. It wasn't often he got to see them interact without the business angle, and even that was seen sparingly. They seemed much more normal this way. "Why did you want it if it's chocolate? You don't like it. ...Doesn't it make you sick?"

"I thought it wouldn't be chocolate for once. And you're always harping on me to socialize more." So even *they* had noticed the lack of normalcy. Remington pushed his bowl away from him and set his chin in his hand. He looked at Michael and asked, "Is it always chocolate for dessert?"

"Usually, but not always."

"Hmph."

"...What's wrong with chocolate?" Michael ventured. He had been involved, again, in the conversation, so he might as well try to be courteous.

"It makes me sick. Literally," Remington said with a nod to Silvermin. "As opposed to him. I do believe he could live off of the stuff."

"I've lived off of worse things than chocolate," Silvermin said without thinking. Michael cringed, and once he had realized what he'd said, Silvermin cringed as well. Remington looked between the two of them curiously. He didn't ask, though.

As predicted, the Rook was thrilled that the two men were leaving early. He pranced around Michael excitedly. The boy just wrapped his arms around himself for warmth. Being out at midnight in January in the woods wasn't a smart idea, but it was the only way he could appease the Rook and get him to stop sleeping inside.

"Once they leave, I don't have to leave you anymore, Michael! Aren't you excited for that?" the Rook chattered on.

"Of course," Michael responded mechanically, shivering. The Rook wasn't put off by the cold temperatures, but he sure was. He only had a coat on, too. He glanced back at the house and pulled the hood up over his head. No one would be awake at this time. Remington always retired early and Silvermin snored, so it was easy to tell when it would be safe to sneak out.

"That didn't *sound* excited." Michael hadn't even noticed the Rook spoke until he hit him in the arm with his wing. "Are you even listening to me?"

"Of course I am. Would I be stupid enough to ignore you?"

"Why are you acting like that?"

"...Like what?"

"Are you cold?" the Rook asked with a dawning look of realization. Michael couldn't help but roll his eyes.

"Yes, I am. Humans are bothered by below zero temperatures."

"I'm bothered, too. I just don't show it. Humans are too

fragile."

"We all can't be like you, Rook."

"I've noticed." Without further warning, the Rook put his arms around Michael and pulled him against his chest. He then wrapped his wings around him, too. "Is this better?"

"…A bit." It blocked most of the breeze, at least, and while the Rook didn't have much body heat to offer, he did offer the mentality of giving it. That probably helped more than anything else did. "…So are we just going to stand here like this? I'll probably fall asleep if we do," Michael threatened.

"Fine then." The Rook immediately released him, stepping away with his arms crossed. "Freeze to death."

"Why are you—"

"Why aren't you excited, Michael? The other two will be gone. It will just be you and me again. Why aren't you glad they're leaving?" The Rook gave him a sidelong glance, eyes narrowed dangerously. Michael suddenly felt colder, if such a thing were possible. "Are you getting attached to them?"

"I—I don't want to cause a fuss. If they are killed, people will come looking for them. That's *all*, I promise."

"I'm wondering, though, Michael. You're spending so much time with them, time that they're taking away from me. I think you *are* getting attached to them. Will I have to take care of them?"

"Rook, you promised. You promised me you wouldn't kill Mr. Silvermin and—"

"*No*, remember?" The Rook advanced on him with a glittering smile. "I only promised not to kill Silvermin. The other one came into the picture unexpectedly. And if I killed him, then obviously I'd have to kill Silvermin too to prevent him from talking, promise or no promise."

"Why can't you just let them leave? They will be gone in a

couple days! We can be here alone from then on—we can leave before next winter—why can't you just let them *live*?!"

"Because, Michael. They're taking you away from me."

Michael lost the argument, but Silvermin and Remington miraculously stayed alive through the rest of the time until they left of their own accord. The Rook laid low until then. The two businessmen packed up their things and restocked the cabin with food for Michael. Silvermin promised to return in a couple weeks' time. Michael bade them both goodbye. Remington laughed as they left.

The Rook hardly waited for them to get out of sight before he took over the house. He tackled Michael, swept him up in his arms, and half-dragged, half-carried him around to each of the rooms. Michael scrabbled for air and balance. The Rook ignored that and concentrated on grinning and babbling and the fact that he and Michael were alone again.

"Come on, come on, let's celebrate! I have my Michael back, all to myself!"

Michael didn't think that really needed celebration, but whatever made the Rook happy. Still holding the boy in a headlock, the Rook rummaged through the cabinets, apparently looking for food. Eventually, he found popcorn, forced Michael to make it, and they settled in on the couch. The Rook kept an arm around his shoulders and glared at him whenever he got up, so for the most part, they spent the night like that.

It was almost nice, too.

The days slowly blurred together, due to Michael's suddenly abnormal sleeping habits. The Rook often woke him and was loathe to let him fall asleep, so he didn't get much actual sleep. Eventually, the Rook gave up on keeping him awake, and made a giant nest in the living room for the boy. It really was a *nest*, too.

"Your bird side is showing," Michael said with a sluggish giggle.

"Shut up and get in here so you can be done sleeping already."

"Thanks," he yawned and crawled into the mess of blankets. The Rook huddled over him, folding his wings over them. Michael couldn't help but think that it really was too much like a bird's nest. Even if it was no different from the usual nighttime arrangements, it looked absolutely absurd in his mind's eye.

It was in the middle of the third night, the night when Michael was finally about to get a good night's sleep, that the door crashed open and they received a very unwelcome visitor.

The Rook was immediately crouched down over the nest, wings outstretched, teeth bared. Michael peered blearily over the edge of the blankets. All he could see was a dim silhouette in the doorway, outlined by the sharp light from the moon on the snow outside. The silhouette's head was tilted back, and he could vaguely see a grin.

"You," the Rook spat.

"I knew you'd kept in contact with the boy. It was just a matter of catching you. It was just a matter of drawing you out into the *open*." The figure spoke with a masculine voice—a voice that was all too familiar to Michael.

"If you knew I was here, why didn't you act sooner? Why didn't you try to confront me?" the Rook said, voice suddenly taking on a taunting tone. He carefully placed himself between the silhouette and Michael. The movement was not lost on either of them.

"Some amount of tact had to be used, don't you think? We

are not all as indiscreet as you, Rook. But now, *now* I finally have you."

"What makes you think—?"

"Michael there. You may be able to outrun me or fly away, but will you be able to get past me with *Michael* to worry about? I am not above using the boy as a weapon against you. It's worked so well in the past, hasn't it?"

"What makes you think I won't just kill you right now? What makes you think you'll get into a position where you can even *touch* him?" The Rook grinned sharply, slowly tensing for a spring. Either the figure before him didn't notice or didn't care.

"If you were going to kill me, don't you think I'd be dead? You don't have the nerve to kill me. ...I, on the other hand, have plenty of nerve to kill you or Michael or whoever I need to in order to get revenge for what you did." The figure stepped into the firelight, hazel eyes flashing as he continued to smile at the Rook. Michael could only stare at him. He could only stare, mouth agape, at Remington.

"I knew I should've killed you when I had the chance," the Rook sneered.

"Yes, you probably should've. Instead, you didn't. That's the fact of the matter, Rook," Remington said with a chuckle. He shrugged and gestured to them both. "...You've really been here the entire time, haven't you? That's so stupid."

"I take it so have you. Which means that I've been here right under your *nose*."

"Aha, you didn't know I was here, either. We were both only grasping at straws, trying to outmaneuver the other, and we have been this close the entire time. Can't you see the irony of the situation?"

"Less irony, and more stupidity. You didn't even realize I was here. Did you *really* think I'd leave Michael?"

"Of course not. We were only using him as bait. I just thought..." he left off thoughtfully, glancing down at his shoes. When he spoke again, he looked back up—at Michael. "Did you ever tell your Rook what I looked like?"

"N-No—he never asked—*what* is going on here?" Being addressed allowed him the courage to finally speak. Remington was back for no apparent reason, and he didn't seem very surprised to find the Rook. The Rook recognized him. Now they were speaking as if he had been looking for the Rook—which meant that Remington had to be another demon. It didn't make sense, but it was the only conclusion that Michael could come to.

Then where did Silvermin fit in? That, bizarrely, was the next thing that came to his mind.

"Yes, Rook, why don't you tell him what's going on here? About how stupid you were and how we were both fooled?" Remington asked smugly.

The Rook, for his part, rolled his eyes. "I thought... I thought if anyone else came I'd be able to sense them. But I wasn't the only one in the dark there, right?"

"What's going on? Who *is* he?"

Both of them turned to Michael in surprise. Remington turned away again, covering his mouth to try to hide a laugh. "Wow, you *are* stupid."

"Michael, he's the one who's been after us. He's the one who killed the Rabbit." Michael looked at Remington with a new eye. At least, until the Rook continued. "He's the Ram."

CHAPTER FOURTEEN

Send My **Condolences** To Good

"*What*?! But you—you killed him! You—Rook, you *tore* off his *head* and—how can he be Mr. Remington?! How can you two have lived this long this close together without *figuring this out*?!"

"The Rook has escaped my detection by sheer virtue of the fact that we're too familiar with one another," Remington—the Ram—said irritably. He crossed his arms over his chest.

"When did I ever say I *killed* him? I wish I had, especially now, but I only stole his head," the Rook added, giving Michael a disdainful look.

"And now you're going to pay for that oversight, for that injustice. I won't make the same mistake, too. I can guarantee it."

With that, the Ram tore the door off its hinges and threw it. The Rook lost a few feathers ducking under it, but otherwise it missed and splintered against the wall behind them. Michael turned to stare at it, aghast. It had been solid wood, after all.

He barely had time to react past that before the Rook was pulling him to his feet, hovering over him with panicky flaps. He yanked him out of the nest and on the other side of the room while the Ram advanced on them. He made a grab for the Rook but missed by centimeters. He then made a second attempt, and missed by a mile. The Rook grinned worriedly.

"Michael, stay out of this one!" he said, not giving the boy another glance. His eyes were fixed only on the Ram. The Ram, for his part, looked around himself disinterestedly. It turned out he was looking for something else to throw. He picked up the couch with one hand and swung it around at the Rook, who clung to the rafters, out of his reach.

"Get down from there and fight me," the Ram called, eyes narrowed in obvious annoyance. The Rook stubbornly shook his head. The Ram looked around for more things to throw—eyes alighting, briefly, on Michael, pressed up against the far wall—and eventually sidled up to the fireplace. He dug his hands into the stone and ripped nearly half of it away from the wall, hurling it at the Rook. The Rook dove out of the way.

Most of the rafters cracked or completely broke while the Rook scooped up Michael in his arms. Behind them, the Ram pried the rest of the fireplace away from the wall. The Rook and Michael broke through the nearest window, ignoring the glass, and tumbled out into the snow.

Michael immediately shivered as he glanced back at the cabin. "We had better—" He barely had time to scramble out of the way as the Ram punched his way through the wall. He strode out into the snow and looked down at the two. He had completely demolished an entire wall of a log cabin, and he hadn't even broken a sweat. Michael turned to the Rook fearfully.

"Ram, why are you mad at me?" the Rook crooned, looking significantly less scared now that he had the open air around him. The Ram snorted. "I left you alive. Your powers are alive and well, so it's not like I stole them from you. All I did was take an itty bitty body part…"

"You stole my *skull*."

"Are you going to take it back?" It almost sounded like a challenge.

"By the time we're done here, you'll wish I had." The Ram gave him a glittering smile and stalked towards him. The Rook took to the air easily, circling above him with a caw-like laugh. "Is this it?! Are you just going to run?"

"I'm not running! Try and *catch* me, Ram!"

"I'm not playing another game with you, Rook! I'm here for revenge, nothing else! I'm here to splinter your bones and carve out your heart with your ribs. No—I'll use your *wings* to do it!" The Ram stopped suddenly. Very slowly, he continued talking, "...No... Actually, Rook, change of plans. I just thought of the *best idea*. See, you took my head, right? Well I know how much you *love* your wings, so maybe I'll just steal them! An eye for an eye, right?! I'll steal your wings for yourself, leave you a broken, bloody mass, and leave you *alive*. You'll never fly again!"

"You'll have to catch me!" the Rook shouted back, arcing higher in the sky. He sounded fearful again, though. Michael silently inched through the snow away from them, shivering, teeth chattering, and wondering how they were going to get away from this alive.

"I can't believe—" the Ram leisurely walked over to the nearest, largest tree, "—you are seriously—" wrapped his arms as much as he could around it, dug his fingers deep into the bark, "—thinking you can get away from me—" and lifted the tree with a grunt, "—you stupid bird." He swung it like a baseball bat, nearly catching the Rook in its topmost branches. He shifted it in his arms and threw it like a spear.

This time, it *did* catch the Rook. Michael's breath hitched when he watched him collapse into the snow. It sent up a flurry of white, obscuring both their views. When it finally settled again, the Rook was caught in the branches and needles as if it was a net, flailing and straining and beating his wings to try to dislodge himself. The Ram let out a hoarse laugh, jumped up onto the edge of the trunk, and walked along its length.

"I'll kill you." The Rook lost his taunt, his challenge. His voice was low and his eyes were hard; Michael knew that look. He wasn't threatening the Ram. He was warning him.

"We've been over this before," the Ram replied patiently. He even added a smile. "You can't kill me, Rook. You simply don't have it in you. Do you?"

The Rook snarled at him, and then made his first and last mistake: he glanced over at Michael. It was only a flicker of the eyes, a fleeting glimpse, but it told the Ram all he needed to know. His smile grew into a wide grin.

"You haven't changed *at all*."

The Rook didn't respond with words, instead growling and hissing at him, clawing at the branches pinning him to the snow. The Ram chuckled and crouched down on one of the nearer branches. The Rook took a swing at him, missing by a hair's breadth.

"…Oh, Rook. Why did it have to come to this? When did you get so soft? If you would've just killed me… If you would just kill me now—but that would hurt your Michael, wouldn't it? You've gone *soft*, Rook." The Ram caught his wrist on the second swing. He snapped it with minimal effort, keeping his smile firmly in place. The Rook didn't react aside from a small wince and continued glaring at him.

"I haven't gone soft. I was just waiting for an opportunity to do this." The Rook grabbed onto the Ram's arm with his free hand. It took just moments for the Ram to break his grip and get away from him, but it seemed that that was all the Rook needed. His power was to steal life, after all.

The Ram wasn't dead, but he had a noticeable sluggishness, and he moved his arm as if it were numb. The Rook, on the other hand, wiggled out of the branches easily now. It seemed as if it had been a lure to get the Ram close. His scratches and even his broken wrist were all gone, only a couple smears of blood to show that he had even been injured.

"Get out of that pathetic human body now," the Ram demanded with a scowl.

The Rook shook his head. "Do you think I'm stupid? I'm not giving up that advantage. Unlike you, I'm just *fine* in this body." He spread his wings and arms wide. The Ram's scowl darkened.

He lunged at the Rook, who jumped and tried to fly out of the way, but was just a bit too slow. The Ram caught him by the ankle and slammed him back down against the ground. Before the Rook could try to get back up or defend himself, he picked him back up, swung him around to gain momentum, and repeated the motion.

The Rook managed to kick him off and took a flying leap for the fallen tree. The Ram tore after him—but ended up skidding to a halt in front of him as he tore off a branch and brandished it like a knife. The tables were turned and the Rook chased the Ram past the tree and out into the forest.

Michael lost sight of them.

It took him a couple moments to process the fact that they were actually *gone*. The fight was still all too audible, with trees cracking and birds shrieking and the occasional shout, but it was muffled and getting farther and farther away. Michael blinked, mouth still agape, and watched as the top of one of the trees suddenly vanished as the Ram undoubtedly pulled it up by the roots.

Remington was the Ram. He had been the Ram the entire time. How was that even *possible*? He didn't put it past their entire race that one could survive his head being ripped off, not anymore, but *still*. Why hadn't the Rook mentioned it before? Especially after the Rabbit was killed—by the *Ram*! Had he known that the entire time? Probably; he had sounded pretty irate after they found her body.

So why hadn't the Ram called Michael out the first time they met? It sounded like he had known all along that he'd been with the Rook, so why not just ask him about it, or hold him hostage or something?

And where did *Silvermin* fit into all of this?

A chill wind brought Michael back to the present. He shivered and wrapped his arms around himself, trudging back through the snow towards the house. Boots would be nice about then. Boots and a coat and the gun that Silvermin kept in his study. It was a rifle mounted on the wall. Michael had seen it a couple times when he'd visit the businessman in there, and while he had no idea whether or not it was real and would work, it was worth a shot.

The Rook was losing, because he didn't want to kill Michael. So it was up to him to try to even the odds a bit.

He pulled on a coat and found his boots, ignoring the way he couldn't feel his feet and their bluish tinge. For good measure, he pulled on a hat, too. Outside, there was more shouting and a loud crack. He heard the distinct sound of the Rook's laugh.

Not a moment later, a tree crashed through the living room. The Rook was wrestling savagely with a branch that pinned him to the trunk of the tree. Michael blinked and backed up in fright. The branch was thrust through the Rook's shoulder and was embedded in the bark beneath him.

"And you thought I couldn't make the shot!" The Ram leapt up onto the roots of the tree, arms crossed smugly.

"When I get this out—"

"Oh, *there* you are Michael!" the Ram interrupted, suddenly looking up at Michael with a dangerous glint in his eye. He looked nothing like Remington anymore. His curly hair was tousled, he had claw marks across one cheek, and he had what could only be described as a slasher smile. He was not a harmless businessman. He never had been. Truly a wolf in sheep's clothing.

The boy wordlessly pressed himself up against the nearest wall. His breath hitched as the Ram stalked towards him. He had a predatory gleam in his eye and the Rook finally caught sight of it when the pale-haired man brushed past him. The Rook swore and started fighting even more violently with the branch.

Shaking hard, Michael dragged himself to his feet. He took all of two steps towards the nearest exit before the Ram was on him, picking him up easily with one hand. Michael's feet swung over the ground as he tore at the Ram's hand, which was clenched around his throat. He couldn't breathe. He dug his nails into the hand as hard as he could, convincing himself that he was even drawing blood—but if there was any pain, it didn't register in the least on the Ram's face.

He held Michael out at arm's length and hopped back up onto the tree trunk. Michael tried kicking him, but the Ram managed to dodge and tighten his grip on his throat. All struggling immediately stopped. Michael's eyelids fluttered as his vision slowly started fading to darkness. His lungs screamed for air, his brain demanded more oxygen, and his heart was the only thing he could hear at that point.

Michael was abruptly dropped.

He gasped for air, tears only then springing to his eyes. He could not get enough air, even now that he had it again. Massaging his throat, he fell back and looked up to see the Rook standing behind the Ram, claws literally at his throat. They were digging in deep enough to form droplets of blood at the tip of each nail. The Ram seemed perfectly composed.

It was only then that Michael realized the Rook was only threatening the Ram with one hand. His shoulder from where the branch had pinned him to the tree was completely mangled, as if he… His eyes widened and he glanced fearfully over at the spot the Rook had previously been. The branch was embedded in the trunk. The Rook had literally torn himself free in order to get to Michael.

He had very nearly lost his arm in the process, too. It hung limply at his side, blood running down it and soaking into the tattered remains of his sleeve.

The Rook's claws dug into the Ram's neck. "You don't touch my Michael."

"Aren't you touchy," the Ram observed. His eyes darted back to Michael's; the Rook's nails dug in even deeper. "I get it. I won't go for him again."

"I'll rip your head off a second time," the Rook breathed, baring his teeth in a feral grin. "Won't that be fun, Ram? Almost as fun as watching you try to take advantage of my Michael!"

"Almost," the Ram agreed weakly. The claws went deeper still, and this time, he winced.

The Rook momentarily released his grip, moving his hand up to hook the Ram under the chin. Michael saw what would happen next: his demonic protector would literally rip the Ram's skull off (for a second time) and that would be the end of the fight.

Instead, the Ram took complete advantage of that split second where the Rook had no hold on him.

His hands clamped down on the Rook's shirt and he flipped him over his head. If it had gone as planned, the Ram would have slammed him down onto Michael's legs and probably would have broken bones in both of them. As it was, the Rook's shirt tore; the sudden shift in weight caused the Ram to lose his balance. He dropped the Rook and slipped off the tree trunk, landing on top of him.

They struggled with each other for a few moments, one of them trying to take control of the fight again, but neither of them quite succeeding. Michael heard the now familiar sound of bones snapping, but every time the Ram managed that, the Rook would merely start stealing more life in order to heal himself.

214

Finally, the Rook managed to roll over into a position where he could throw the Ram off with his wings. He shakily got to his feet. He was actually looking better than he had been earlier, though he could still barely use his arm. His wings were half-curled around his shoulders; it was a defensive stance. He could steal life, but not enough to kill the Ram, and the fight was starting to wear on him.

The Ram was looking drained, too, which was the only upside to the situation. He was barely standing, and even then, he was swaying. He threw out a hand to steady himself on the fallen tree. The Rook grinned at him weakly. The Ram bared his teeth at him in response, dug his fingers into the bark, and ripped off a sizable piece. He threw it at the Rook, but it missed easily as the Rook sidestepped it. This repeated several times before the Ram finally gave up on it with a soft growl.

"You… won't be able to… kill me like this… Rook," he panted, lurching towards him. The Rook stepped away from him. He watched the Ram curiously, slowly uncurling his wings from around him.

"I seem to be doing a halfway decent job of it," he replied. He sounded much better than the Ram.

"There are… two ways, idiot…" The Rook paid for his carelessness around the Ram when the latter managed to grab his wing. He pulled on it, snapping bones and feathers like twigs. The Ram smirked. "I'm just… tired, not out of this yet, Rook."

"Oh yeah, there are two ways, aren't there?" The Rook, injured wing folded tightly against him, jumped up onto the tree and backed away from the Ram. He glanced over at Michael, then back down at his enemy. "Guess I'll have to end this the old-fashioned way."

As the Ram laboriously got back onto the tree and tottered after him, falling twice but getting angrier as he went, the Rook pulled out the branch that had pinned him to the trunk just moments earlier. He pulled it out just as the Ram lunged at him. His hands closed around air as the Rook ducked under his grasp.

The Rook stuck the branch under his arm and grabbed the Ram, as he passed him, by his hair. He dragged him out of the half-destroyed cabin, only pausing once to look back at Michael. "...Want to know how to kill a demon, Michael? Come out here and I'll show you."

Michael didn't trust the situation, but he slowly followed them back out into the snow. There was something in the Rook's tone that told him not to disobey right then. He was completely serious, and while he had a hard grin, it was too forced for it to be natural. The Rook was angry, as angry as he'd ever seen him, and hurt and glaring down at the Ram with all of the ferocity he could muster.

"There are two ways, but everyone else can only use one of them. I'm special because I can kill others in both ways. I can take away their life, though I can't just grab at it like I've been trying." He looked down his nose at the Ram as he threw him to the ground. The Ram rolled over but before he could get up, the Rook placed a foot on his chest to pin him. The Ram silently snarled and grabbed his ankle.

Half of his leg and foot were shattered before he could retract it. Michael felt sick; he could see several pieces of bone sticking out of the dark fabric of his pants, and blood was starting to seep into it and run down his foot. It was already dripping onto the Ram's chest.

The Rook didn't react past curling his lip. "The second way to kill a demon is to rip out their heart and eat it. Which I'm going to demonstrate *right now*." He pulled out the sharp branch again, holding it over his head like an overly long dagger.

Bang.

The Rook's eyes widened and he took a half step forward, grip slackening on the branch. There was suddenly blood—more of it—staining his shirtfront. He turned around, but there was another loud report and this time, there was a visible spray of blood as he was hit in the throat.

He dropped the branch altogether this time, hands flying up to his neck. The Rook stumbled forward, tripped over the Ram, and fell down. The Ram sat up and chuckled weakly in the direction of the new assailant. Michael unconsciously copied the action.

"About time... Silvermin."

Silvermin lowered the rifle, sighing. In the cold, his breath came out as a cloud of mist. He ran a wrist over his eyes as he sauntered closer, though he was obviously going to stay at a healthy distance. "Looks like you've had a bloody rough time of this, Rem." He might have been saying 'Rem', or he might have been saying 'Ram'. It was difficult to tell with his accent, but it made Michael wonder how he hadn't seen it before.

"M-Mr.—Silvermin—*why*?!"

"Rem and I have a business deal," he stated in a cold little monotone. He took another cautious step forward, still pointing the rifle at the Rook.

"He's not dead yet... The deal's not over yet..." The Ram painstakingly got to his feet, hands on his knees for support. The Rook coughed and dripped scarlet into the snow, struggling to get back up. The Ram noticed this and, taking a steeling breath, stomped over to him. He placed a foot squarely on the Rook's back and pushed down.

"G-Get off of me—fight me like a real—" the Rook snarled into the snow, flailing with his wings in an effort to beat the Ram off. He only succeeded in flicking droplets of blood everywhere and annoying him.

"Plans changed… Rook. I am going to kill you now. But first… I am going to rip off your wings… and then I'll hurt you. Once you're begging me for death… You'll receive your death—after you watch Michael's." Silvermin grimaced and looked at Michael. He opened his mouth to speak, but the Ram continued. "You have no idea what it felt like to get my skull just… ripped off like that. But you'll have something similar, I think, with your wings."

He pushed down on the Rook's spine with his foot, bent down, and grabbed a wing in each hand. Then, he pulled.

CHAPTER FIFTEEN

The **Horror** Of Our Love

The psychologist flinched at the tap on the glass behind him. He turned and scowled over his shoulder—momentarily perplexing his patient—and stood up. "Excuse me. I'll be right back, Michael."

"...Okay," came the passive reply.

He pushed himself away from the table and marched to the door, threw it open, and closed it carefully behind him. He would've liked to slam it, but as his patient (like most of the patients in the asylum) had a rather fragile state of mind, loud noises weren't a good idea.

"I don't know what you were talking about." The room had one single occupant, who was perched on a chair with his nose pressed against the one-way mirror. The psychologist narrowed his eyes at him and didn't respond. The man grinned up at him, nodding back at his patient through the glass. "This is *gold*! You say there's a story in this?"

"You've heard it yourself. It's been two years now, and every time anyone asks about what happened, that's the story we get. More or less."

"More or less?"

"A couple minor things change from narrative to narrative. At least the ending has stayed constant now. When we first—"

"It's constant now? So what we just heard was the ending? Could use a bit of work, but it's decent stuff. Great fight towards the end. Could make a kickass book. Real goddamn great book. Hell, even a movie."

"Stop interrupting me and *listen*, will you?!" the psychologist snapped, suddenly aggressive. The man in the chair took notice and backed down. "That kid out there is a patient. A patient in an asylum. Does that even *register* with you?! Oh, I knew it was a bad idea to invite you along..."

"Eh, but you've had this one for a couple years now, haven't you? And hasn't, uh, *Michael* was it?" He glanced out at the padded room with its sole occupant. He didn't finish his initial question and instead continued with a different, more defensive train of thought. "Look, you knew we were looking for things to make a book with, and you know we have all of the politics of it out of the way. We just need one that's been getting cured. Is cured. Whichever makes a better story. But this—*this*! This is much better than we'd anticipated!"

"I was afraid of that," the psychologist murmured, though his guest didn't hear him.

"...made up a whole goddamn *culture*! And it's been the same exact story—more or less!—for the last two years! You can't beat that, you really can't. This'll be great. A whole goddamn culture! God, I can't believe it. That was a really kickass story, I'm not going to lie. A book like that would sell. It'd sell even more if they knew it was a *crazy* who came up with it—"

"Can you at least pretend to care a whit about the person on the other side of that glass? The *human life* you want to sacrifice to the media in the name of finding a good story?! You—You don't even know the meaning behind that story!" The anger was back. It had been two years since the psychologist had met with this patient, but after hearing the harrowing events leading up to that fateful meeting, he'd become attached. It wasn't a good thing, but it had happened nonetheless.

The man scratched at his stubble, eyes downcast. "So... tell me then. Tell me what actually happened."

"Two years ago, there was a shipwreck. It killed all but four or so. One of them died on the island they washed up on, so there was three. A middle-aged man who had never had more than ten minutes of contact with a child before, a college-aged girl, and a young boy.

"Eventually, after too many days of no food, apparently they snapped and... And..."

"Killed and ate 'im, right...?" the man said, as gently as he ever could.

The psychologist collapsed into the nearest chair, burying his face in his hands. "You have to understand the mindset that that trial put them all in. They were literally starving to death. You can't comprehend—*I* can't comprehend it. But damn it all, I've come as close as anyone, I suppose."

"Then what? Something must've led from Point A to Point B besides cannibalism."

"Couldn't you at least pretend to have a heart!?"

"I'll work on that. Please, continue with your story." He waved his hand dismissively, though at least he looked attentive.

"It had been Tuesday's idea to eat each other. And then they, well, did just that... And not three hours after they ate him, rescue came. *Three hours*. If they had lasted three hours longer, Michael wouldn't have had to die. ...Could you actually *imagine* that?! Three hours. *Three hours*. It was all in vain. They killed and ate a small boy—and it was wasted."

"So... She feels guilty? That why she calls herself that?"

"Her psyche was completely shattered by the time I met with her for the first time. She really believed she *was* Michael. I believe she was trying to make up for his wasted death by sacrificing herself to become him. She wanted to give him the life they deprived him of."

"Wait, I still don't get this. There's three of them, and she suggests cannibalism, and then they *do* the cannibalism, and then rescue shows up three hours later?"

"Shut up and *imagine* it. Imagine that was you on the other side of that glass. How would *you* feel?" he said in a strained voice, not daring to look at his patient anymore.

"...Okay, okay. I get it now, a bit. What happened to the other person, the man?" his guest asked curiously, tilting his head.

"He was the one who took most of the punishment. Since he was not declared insane, he went to court and was given what amounts to a life sentence. In a way, she gave him a bit more of a life, too." The psychologist didn't know much about Silvermin's punishment, having only seen the documents secondhand and only the ones that directly pertained to his patient.

"So... How *exactly* does that story fit into all of it?"

"She had always wanted to tell a story," the psychologist said softly. "She said she had always told him stories. Her mother was a librarian. She grew up loving stories, and had always wanted to tell one. So that, coupled with her extreme guilt and her desire to give Michael the life they took from him, she created this. She honestly believes she *is* Michael, that this happened to her, and while she is coming around, she's going to have problems with this for the rest of her life. The lines between fiction and reality are too blurred."

The man whistled lowly. "Well damn. Never would've imagined it from a little thing like her."

"In her story, nearly five years have passed. She's been telling that story since the second night after she came here. She managed to give him five more years of life in just two days."

"You say she's getting better?"

"She doesn't throw things or start screaming if you accidentally call her Tuesday, at least." A guard had made that mistake on the first night of her arrival. He still had the scars across his face from where she had tried to claw his eyes out. "Call her Michael."

"So she takes over this little boy's life... Doesn't he have any family? What do they—"

The psychologist looked down at his hands, folded in his lap. "Michael Sante never existed."

"*What*?! Are you shitting me, seriously?! You just said so yourself—!"

"Tuesday had never learned much of anything about the little boy on the island with her. Her memories of her time are warped. I doubt she really even interacted with him at all. His name was actually Zachary Jones, and he was ten years old when he was killed. His immediate family died on the boat. She's never had anyone to correct her, so she created Michael to try to help her live with the guilt. I highly doubt Zachary acted anything like Michael."

"I could buy that," his guest replied suspiciously, still regarding him with narrowed eyes, "But what about the Rook and all them? She still invented a whole goddamn culture. In a day. …She certainly got that story she wanted to make."

"The Rook and all of the accompanying demons who tortured Michael were a way for her to try to come to terms with what had happened. She wanted it to be someone else's fault, so she created the Rook. The Rook wanted to hurt Michael, so he could be blamed for it all. He was merely a defense mechanism her subconscious put in place to prevent itself from being ripped apart by her conscious mind—and story. No matter how guilty she felt or feels, even now, she doesn't *want* to feel guilty. No human does. She still wanted to blame someone else for everything."

"It'll make a damn fine story. You think Michael would be okay with it?" His mind was still on business. The psychologist had to wonder how much of the truth actually penetrated his mind, or if he ever thought about anything or anyone other than himself.

"I've asked her about it several times, but she's never given me a definite answer. I believe, with more rehabilitation and if she were to ever fully come to terms with what had happened, if she could return to society, you could ask her then."

"How about I meet her now and ask her now? If we got some sort of answer now, I could go back and talk it over with a couple of others. This is fine material. Maybe we could get the rights to it if all else fails..." He scratched at his chin again. "You *said* she wanted to make a story, so I could make it happen for her—"

"You can't meet her right now. Her mind is always most fragile when she finishes the story," the psychologist said at once, unable to help the protectiveness from slipping into his voice.

His guest noticed. With a grin, he told him, "I'll be careful, I promise. The word Tuesday will not leave these lips."

"It's not just that. You're loud, you're brash, and most importantly, you're a stranger to her. No good whatsoever would come from you meeting with her now. At a later date, *maybe*."

"Fine, fine. Any chance I could talk to you for a while longer? Duck out of this. She's looking sort of antsy, so you might want to wrap it up anyway." He gestured uselessly at the patient on the other side of the glass. True enough, the silver charm bracelet was being tugged at again. There were scars around her wrist from the movement repeated so many times, but trying to take it from her was nearly as bad as calling her Tuesday instead of Michael. "Go put her to bed. Let her get some sleep."

"...Fine."

The psychologist bade his patient goodnight, and a single guard escorted her back to her room. She was much more docile now. He couldn't help but wonder if she *would* like to make a book.

Tuesday sat on the bed, leaning against the cool wall. There was a single window in her room, high up and barred over. She wrung the charm bracelet around her wrist, not feeling it. Her wrist had gone numb from the movement long ago.

There had been someone else listening in on that story, she was sure of it. She was only told to recount what had happened when something else had happened—or something was going to happen. At least her psychologist was nice about it.

She pulled her knees up to her chest and set her forehead on them. She hardly noticed it when the bed near her feet suddenly sunk down, as if someone had sat on it.

"They were right." She looked up, dully, at the voice. He was back again. He turned and looked at her, grinning lazily. "That would make a great book. Think, all of those humans who would get to enjoy the story! All those humans would get to hear what happened to you. Doesn't that make you happy? You'd finally get to make your very own story, your own book."

Tuesday shut her eyes tight, but didn't hide her face. She didn't dare. She couldn't stop herself from listening to him, though. "I... I don't..." She looked at him again, eyes glazed. He didn't seem to have heard her.

He shifted so that he was fully facing her. He was dressed in one of the guard uniforms, wings folded passively behind him. She couldn't help but wonder how he had got in this time; she kept *telling* them to keep him away from her. It never seemed to work, however.

"I—don't—want—" she choked out, closing her eyes once more. If she didn't look at him, he'd go away. If she pretended to herself that he didn't exist, he'd leave her alone...

"Well, was it worth it?" the Rook asked with a dark smile. "Was your story worth losing everything, Michael?"

And so, it all ended with the Rook, too.

And now, for a preview of the second book in the trilogy:

THE RAM

This time, it started with the Ram.

Tuesday had been out of the asylum for a little over a year. The Rook left her alone more once she had left the place, usually only visiting every couple of weeks. It almost convinced her she was on the road back to sanity.

Her psychologist said that the Rook wasn't real, that he never had been. None of them had been real. They were just figments and products of her guilty conscience. She just had to concentrate on that fact and take solace in it.

So then what was the demon who was haunting her, calling her Michael, leaving scars all over her body and psyche?

It had been three weeks since she had last seen the Rook. He had only stopped in to torture her a bit, breaking her bathroom mirror when he had slammed her head against it. The mirror was still broken, and the cuts on her face were mostly healed; how had an invention of her deranged imagination done *that*?

She sighed and ran a brush through her wet hair. Life was mundane in the real world. She didn't prefer college, the island, or the asylum to it, but it didn't make it any less unpleasant. She could only get part time work with a single year of college education, but thankfully, she could support herself with it. Well, the pay from that, life insurance from her parents, and book sales. The latter two arrived at her doorstep in monthly checks; she didn't know who was managing her finances, but they did it well, and she got by.

There was suddenly a very loud, insistent knocking on her front door. It successfully pulled her from her thoughts and back out into reality once more.

Tuesday scowled and pulled the towel tighter around herself. "Just a minute!" she called down the hall, finishing brushing her hair as she did so. She scrambled for her clothes as the banging continued. Whoever it was—had she been expecting company?—really wanted in.

Was it the Rook?

She pulled a shirt over her head, took one last look at the broken mirror, and trotted down the hall to answer it. She wasn't expected anyone, at least no one that she remembered. And one didn't get too many unexpected guests when living on the top floor of the apartment building. The knocking intensified—until it stopped altogether.

Tuesday paused in the hallway, gripping the frame of the doorway. Had her guest just left? Why had it stopped? She took a cautious step forward, but she was only greeted by more silence. That was a little alarming. She may have been paranoid, but it didn't mean that it wasn't weird.

Suddenly, her front door flew clean off its hinges. It skidded to a halt in front of her feet. Eyes wide, Tuesday looked up at the silhouette in the doorway.

Though she had never actually seen him before in her life, she recognized him immediately from the Rook's description of him. Pale curly hair, hazel eyes, and it all came with a glare that could peel paint. "You're Tuesday, then. I'm here to talk about your *book*," the Ram spat.

She could only stare at him. She didn't even hear him. The Ram, the Ram, the Ram—he was the Rook's nemesis, his enemy, his killer in her story. He was Remington, he was a fake businessman, he was a character in *The Rook*.

He was *real*.

Which meant that, by association, the Rook himself was real as well. It hadn't been in her mind. None of it had been in her mind. It hadn't been her mind torturing her; it had been a demon. A real, live demon. She hadn't done all those things to herself like her psychologist told her and scolded her for. The

Rook had done them to her. The Rook was real. The Ram was real. Everyone else was real.

Tuesday pitched backward in a dead faint.

Made in the USA
Lexington, KY
22 August 2012